I0564681

The Mind Reels

Also by Fredrik deBoer

The Cult of Smart
How Elites Ate the Social Justice Movement

The Mind Reels

Fredrik deBoer

COFFEE HOUSE PRESS
Minneapolis
2025

Copyright © 2025 by Fredrik deBoer
Cover design by Kyle G. Hunter
Book design by Rachel Holscher

Coffee House Press books are available to the trade through our primary distributor, Consortium Book Sales & Distribution, cbsd.com or (800) 283-3572. For personal orders, catalogs, or other information, write to info@coffeehousepress.org.

Coffee House Press is a nonprofit literary publishing house. Support from private foundations, corporate giving programs, government programs, and generous individuals helps make the publication of our books possible. We gratefully acknowledge their support in detail in the back of this book.

All rights reserved. No part of this book may be used or reproduced in any manner for the purpose of training artificial intelligence technologies or systems.

LIBRARY OF CONGRESS CATALOGING-IN PUBLICATION DATA

Names: deBoer, Fredrik author
Title: The mind reels / Fredrik deBoer.
Description: Minneapolis : Coffee House Press, 2025.
Identifiers: LCCN 2025005980 (print) | LCCN 2025005981 (ebook) |
    ISBN 9781566897372 paperback | ISBN 9781566897389 epub
Subjects: LCGFT: Psychological fiction | Novels
Classification: LCC PS3604.E23395 M56 2025 (print) |
    LCC PS3604.E23395 (ebook) | DDC 813/.6—dc23/eng/20250331
LC record available at https://lccn.loc.gov/2025005980
LC ebook record available at https://lccn.loc.gov/2025005981

PRINTED IN THE UNITED STATES OF AMERICA

32 31 30 29 28 27 26 25   1 2 3 4 5 6 7 8

For Eun Hae

Your eyes, rampant as an open city . . .

—*Maya Angelou*

The Mind Reels

One

Alice was born in Oklahoma but not on the plains, growing up on a cul-de-sac next to an office park in a stretch of land that, she felt quite sure, had never seen a covered wagon. Her daddy sold auto parts but couldn't change a tire and her mother was a mother until Alice was six and then got a job at the public library.

"I work at a library but I'm not a librarian," her mother would say, "and they'll never let me forget it."

Alice never forgot it either; she learned, at a formative age, the pain of being somewhere without being something, or someone.

As a child she liked life well enough. Her parents got along by not talking to one another but still held hands under the table when they went to the diner, and as long as Alice caught them doing this her home felt at peace. She had no siblings and so dreamed of a sister, another girl her age yet somehow not her twin, who in her fantasies would plait her hair with the strong and gentle hands of an adult. Alice had a little pink bike with streamers and she would peddle around what her father called their "neighborhood," which extended no farther than the five little tract houses that ringed their street.

"She's fine," her neighbors would say as she pedaled by. "She's just fine."

She did well enough in school and her mother would tell all her friends that "someday, she'll spoil her mother!" colored with an affected laugh to let everyone know she was joking but insistently enough that Alice knew she needed it to be true. Alice was cared for in all things, never pampered but wanting for nothing, loved just enough to know what love was. There was no great trauma in her early life, no beatings, no sexual abuse, just the steady accumulation of American days.

And yet she emerged into adolescence disturbed nonetheless, traumatized without trauma. There were footprints on her mind where no one had trod.

During playtime one day a boy she did not like handed Alice a crude drawing he had made of her, complete with pigtails she had never worn and a dress of neon green.

"You've got chinky eyes," said the boy as she gazed down at his handiwork.

"I'm just white," said Alice.

"You have chinky eyes," he said again, in a tone that suggested he was passing on wisdom from above. She folded the picture up and took it home and hid it in a book; it meant less than nothing to her but she caressed it as though she treasured it and hid it under a loose floorboard where she would have put the things she treasured had she ever treasured anything. When her mother found it years later, Alice pretended that she had drawn it herself.

Middle school was a pointless collection of gray but cheerful days. She got her period and blood stained her shorts in gym class but somehow her peers never said a cruel word; she kept learning that the world was bitter but full of kindness. That night her mother apologized again and again for the conversation they were always meant to have but didn't.

Alice was never popular in high school, but she was kind and that kindness was rewarded by her peers, who treated her as someone who stood outside of the hierarchy, who lived to putter around the people who mattered and be her own kind self, and they rewarded her with compliments of her plain clothes and features, invitations to parties, rides home from football games. There was a part of her that knew she was being condescended to but she didn't care. The form of acceptance was enough, the letter of the law sufficient. She picked her way through classes like a discerning shopper, absorbing the information that interested her and none that didn't. She got an A in geometry and a C+ in Algebra II, as the former came with pictures and the latter did not. She was the opposite of an unrealized genius; everyone was modestly satisfied by her performance, and not a single soul ever talked about her greater potential, not even her parents. She floated up to the level of B+ advanced mediocrity she was destined to reach, and no higher. In all things she put her head down and marched unwaveringly into the unexceptional spaces everyone had predicted she would occupy. As a senior in high school, this was enough and she was content.

She cried when she was rejected by all of her reach schools but they were the tears of someone who knew that all things were falling into their proper places. She had sworn to her mother that she was never going to go to the University of Oklahoma, that she would sooner set straight off for LA to become an actress than go to OU. That she had never acted a day in her life and harbored no interest in doing so was beside the point. Her mother would merely hum along to a hymn from her childhood and tell her, "Your part is to be what you'll be," which would have sounded wise had she not always followed it up with "like the song, baby, like the song." As was foretold, her father wound up sending a deposit to Norman in March of Alice's senior year. That night she celebrated, or mourned, by letting a persistent and not unattractive boy fuck her in the back seat of her hand-me-down SUV, discarding her virginity like an unwanted gift on the curb.

At her graduation her mother cried and her father gave her flowers that looked more like those that he might lay on her coffin. Under her gown and dress she wore lace panties she had bought in Austin on a trip with some friends; they had stopped in Chickasaw territory and bought some shrooms but after eating them they sat around the motel for hours and felt nothing. She went to the overnight sober graduation party and found that she was among the coolest people there, a condition she always found deeply uncomfortable, a condition that gave her hives. After half-heartedly enjoying the Velcro wall there, with a girl from her childhood gymnastics class, she went out the back door with an amiable stoner and his girlfriend; she was vaguely native, as many girls in the area were, had a labret piercing, and was known to have had an abortion. As they drove to a party in the stoner's car the cool girl offered her a drag from her cigarette, which made Alice lightheaded, and they laughed about how pointless and empty life seemed.

When she got to the party Alice was relieved to feel that she was just cool enough to be there and be comfortable, in the bottom quarter or so of the coolest people present but sufficiently secure in her position. Again her fundamental friendliness went a long way. She was invited to smoke weed by a prominent lieutenant of one of her school's queen bees, a girl who was surely planning to ascend to queen bee status herself when she got to college in the fall. But she was sweet to Alice and laughed when Alice choked and was excited that it was Alice's first time. It was not, not her first or second or tenth time smoking weed, but she went along with the story because the girl had so quickly brought Alice into her circle without fuss and laughed without embarrassment as she got high. Alice let another boy fuck her that night, but this one was a little older and more committed and the weed helped her to concentrate enough that she actually enjoyed it. Afterward he drew him toward her and she rested her head on her chest. She was bored but knew boys needed that sort of thing, and she signed his yearbook while he put his clothes back on.

She drank Coors Light and sucked up Jell-O shots and got too drunk and was taken care of by a sweet chubby cheerleader who was a beloved member of student council and who was said to have given half the soccer team head. The chubby girl cooed as Alice tried and failed to throw up in the bathroom; the feeling of her running her hand through Alice's hair reminded Alice of her maternal grandmother, who had been dead for ten years.

She got home the next morning while her mother was at church. She stank of smoke and stumbled up the steps to the tract house where her father was diligently toying with mulch in the side yard and there was no doubt he saw her and comprehended where she had been and what she had been up to, but he kept his head down and only nodded at her, then studied the mulch, and she knew he would not tell her mother. Later that day she went to Walmart with a friend to buy sheets and a hamper for college. The boy from the party texted her a photo of his abs and she showed it to her friend and they laughed and laughed in the swimsuit aisle, but somehow that night she found herself bent over the arm of the couch at his parent's house, and she pretended to come until he fingered her and she actually did come. He told her he was going to Northwestern. She saw him off and on for a few more weeks that summer but soon got bored. Eventually she told him she was leaving the next week even though she wasn't due on campus for a month and a half. A few weeks after that he drunkenly texted to say that he was in love with her; when she didn't respond he called her a slut.

They held a graduation party in the backyard. Alice sat under a rented canopy tent with her cousins and had the same conversations they always had. Her uncle, a notorious drunk, gave her a roll of quarters for the campus washing machines. ou used a card system in the laundry and the change was quite useless to Alice but she was moved all the same, and she hugged her uncle tight. That day she clutched the quarters in her hand while she dutifully thanked relatives she didn't like for cards stuffed with individual tens and twenties. The quarters shifted around in the roll but as a unit it felt sturdy and though her hand sweated in the Oklahoma summer heat the roll felt cool and she knew she would never have survived the party without it. Years later that uncle would put a bullet into his temple at a roadside motel.

Somehow her mother knew that Alice had started having sex. There was no confrontation, just a series of increasingly pointed asides about choices and boys. Alice folded clothes next to her mother and let these comments flow by her, not listening, staring out the window at a peculiar break in the clouds where the gray-blue sky stood out in stark relief. Her thoughts had been accelerating and she kept idly noticing this fact and then forgetting. This understanding—that her attention was being appropriated by thoughts that raced out in front of her, unbidden and uncontrolled—itself drifted in and out of her mind like a movie she kept meaning to sit down with and then forgot about every time she had the time to watch it. Surely these were simply the stirrings of late adolescence. Eventually she smoked weed again and found herself incapacitated, glued to a chair, thoughts doubling back on themselves in an infinite regress, and all of them pointing back at her, exposing her, revealing every lie she had ever told to the floor and ceiling and walls. The sounds around her seemed to double back on themselves, too, like cackling birds, and she stared and stared straight ahead until someone said something to her, and she responded too quickly and she knew that everyone knew.

Alice had a job lifeguarding that summer, an essential element of her projected college finances, but she called out more days than she went in. When she did go in she would sit on a chair and imagine all the children going under at once. The other guards would mill around and tan and laugh and she would dutifully attend "parties" of a half-dozen people drinking beer in an apartment on a three-month summer rental. When she would go off shift she would hide out in the handicapped stall and rake her inner thighs with tweezers until they were raw and bleeding. By the end of the summer she had failed to turn up so consistently that she only earned $1,845 and her boss told her not to bother to apply the next summer.

Her parents drove her up to Norman and she met her roommate, a sweet gangly Thai girl named Clara. When Clara first spoke Alice was filled with dread at the prospect of her mother commenting on the girl's lack of an accent, but to her immense relief the conversation was never less than pleasant. The two new arrivals giggled softly throughout their first hours together, the quiet laughter of those who would prefer not to be seen. They had not coordinated very well and found themselves with two mini fridges. For an agonizing minute her father impressed on Clara that she could sell hers for a good price on the internet, until Alice's mother intervened and brought her shame to a close.

An hour later and her parents were piling at last into their old Ford Bronco. Her father pressed $200 into Alice's hand in lieu of a hug; her mother wept and kissed her on the lips. Once again declining their invitation to take her and Clara to the Sonic Drive-In, Alice watched with relief as her parents motored away from campus. That first night was to be the fourth she had ever spent on her own. She found Clara to be bright and friendly and shy, and she was secretly pleased that, like her, Clara was not the kind of girl who would ever be considered hot. They wandered campus and some boys hooted at them and Alice pretended to be offended. It was too hot out and at times she felt overwhelmed but Clara's steadiness comforted her and that vast campus seemed to her to contain all of the possibility that could be wrung out of the human world.

They returned to their cramped dorm room and Clara talked about her boyfriend while Alice fumbled with her new laptop. Alice fell asleep to the sound of a makeup tutorial that Clara was watching on her iPhone. Though they had done nothing to decorate yet their dorm seemed warm and safe to Alice, the kind of place she would like to return to after walking through a thunderstorm. It was in that room that Alice would first go insane.

Two

Alice found herself in the familiar position of being the shoulder for a friend to cry on. She and Clara went to a Halloween party at a house some upperclassmen rented off campus. Clara was dressed as Jasmine from *Aladdin*; Alice didn't think she had the tits for it but she thought her stomach looked hot and she told Clara as much a dozen times, a reflexive compliment but a deeply sincere one. Alice was a cat, black leggings and a black top as sheer as she dared, cheap black cat ears and cute little whiskers drawn on her face in eyeliner, Clara's black kohl. It smeared in just the way that Alice had hoped for, and when she looked in the mirror she saw what she so rarely did: the kind of girl who would be noticed walking into a party. While she and Clara waited for the shuttle, Alice was noticed by shamelessly staring boys, they both were, and as is the habit of the young she felt grateful for a night that felt sweaty and alive.

They arrived at the house and found, happily, that they were still being noticed and appreciated. Alice had worried that the party would be dead but it was livelier than expected and the ratio was better, too, something like four sweaty boys to every one well-manicured girl. She'd figured there would be ten dudes for every chick. The ones who'd rented the house were theater majors; the party tasted of the desperation of people who needed to be seen having a good time, but the punch went down easily enough and the music was surprisingly tolerable and Alice's sexy cat costume was doing its job, presenting a fairly convincing impression of cleavage.

Alice had spent the first six weeks of classes aggressively pursuing a boy in her freshman writing class only to see him making out with a handsome townie outside of a diner at 2:00 a.m. That disappointment was fleeting, but the desired to get fucked was not. She was trying to decide how low her standards were at present, whether they were really low enough to sleep with a theater major. It was Halloween, after all, when sweet plain ordinary girls like her were allowed to whore out a little. The bigger problem was Clara.

Clara was now firmly her second best friend; her first best, Sadie, was off at USC and would FaceTime Alice when she was drunk, which was every night. Sadie was hotter than Alice and freer spirited and had lost her virginity when they were fourteen. But Sadie also quietly hated herself, and ever since they grew close at seven years old, Alice had known that she must serve as Sadie's ballast. Sadie needed Alice and Alice needed to be needed, and they had settled into a mutually nurturing equilibrium for so long that the nights that ended with Alice quietly cooing into her cellphone to placate a distraught Sadie felt like home. Now Sadie was in LA, a place that conjured images of every kind of peril in Alice's mind, and Alice was not there to worry over her, to help her mend all the little wounds wrought by Sadie's own carelessness and the world's. Alice was aware that there was something selfish in the way she had doted over Sadie, but there was no question that Sadie needed her, and now she was very far away.

Clara presented another opportunity for Alice to play mother, or martyr. Two months together was enough time for Alice to see the cracks in Clara's façade. She was authentically kind, genuinely shy. But Clara was also callous, at times, guilty of the kind of clumsy meanness that's often bred into the shy, who tend to want intimacy only on their own terms. Alice got used to spending hour after hour talking to Clara as they lay in their beds, sharing their secret thoughts, only to find her cold and distant in the morning. Clara was considering taking a Thai first name, feeling more and more that the Western name she had grown up with was becoming a mark of shame. Alice had no opinion on this matter but found that Clara returned to it so relentlessly that she could murmur the encouragement Clara sought by rote, with no investment of feeling. It struck Alice that anyone could have done the same, with minimal preparation, and for all the appreciation Clara showed afterward, it might as well have been a stranger who'd put in the time.

Still, their friendship was fine, and as both of them were neat and accommodating, living together was easy. The trouble was that Clara had cheated on her boyfriend, in fact gave up her virginity to a tall white local of a kind Alice knew too well. He was the sort to tell everyone that he was "corn-fed" and to accentuate his drawl despite being in every sense a conventional suburban teenager with no real regional identity. Clara sent Alice his Instagram and she had to admit he was cute. She only met him in person once and she found he had a certain dopey charm. When Alice warned Clara that she was getting too close to him, Clara denied it, but ten days later she was weeping in their room because she had allowed him to take her virginity at 11:45 a.m. on a Tuesday morning, after class.

"I thought it would feel like the world stopped," she sobbed, "but it just hurt."

Clara's boyfriend was Filipino. For reasons Alice could not understand, Clara felt that it was a greater betrayal that she had cheated on him with a white man.

"Just don't tell him anything," said Alice. "Just tell the new guy to delete your number and forget this all happened."

Clara resisted but eventually acquiesced to this wisdom. To Alice's dismay, she also fell back into bed with the white boy a few days later, then again, and in short order Alice was advising her to do the opposite.

"You have to come clean," she said. Clara responded by hanging out with friends without asking Alice along, a subtle nod to the fact that she had been more socially successful. This would be Clara's primary lever of control in what would prove to be a short and broken and beautiful friendship, leaving Alice out to emphasize the fact that Clara had other options while Alice did not. Alice's lever was to go silent. "I'll break up with him over Thanksgiving break," said Clara. Alice didn't see much sense in this plan, but she knew that nothing she could say to Clara would be constructive. In the end it didn't matter; somehow the boyfriend found out what was happening and Alice sat outside of their front door and heard Clara heave and sob into the phone as he berated and dumped her. The corn-fed boy stopped returning her texts a week or two later. Then more tears and sobs and stalking him on social media, which Alice put a stop to with the sort of firm and kind intervention at which she excelled. One night when Clara had finally stopped weeping, lying on Alice's lap on her tiny dorm twin bed, Alice stroked her hair and cooed that the good news was that now they were both single. As she had hoped, her roommate let out a howl of freedom.

And so Clara talked incessantly about the upcoming party and about meeting boys and Alice became more and more convinced that she would spend the party looking after her. She worried and worried the day before, but as they got ready Clara appeared composed and untroubled. Which left Alice now feeling a little unmoored, at a theater major party, watching young actors overemote as they played a drinking game. Their gangly awkwardness and desire to be seen bothered her. She glanced longingly at a tall and rangy upperclassman whose girlfriend patrolled him like a Rottweiler guarding a toddler in the backyard.

"Drink," Clara kept saying, pouring more punch into Alice's cup. "Drink."

On some level she would have loved to get drunk, perhaps even wasted, and again the desire to lie under some energetic boy as he pounded away made her wet. The trouble was that she was too preoccupied to drink, or to flirt. Preoccupied with everything, with whatever images came sauntering through the swinging saloon doors of her brain. The truth was, though she was largely succeeding at suppressing her own understanding of the fact, in recent weeks a tide of racing thoughts had risen up within her again. As she knew even less about psychology than she did about love or regret she had no vocabulary with which to describe this problem to herself, much less to others. Presently she was pondering her calculus final and Clara's precise level of inebriation and the possibility of getting fucked and whether she should go out back to where the people were smoking weed even though smoking any herself seemed like a terrible idea and also about getting fucked and how the corn-fed boy had recently liked several of her pictures on Instagram and the meaning of loyalty and she thought about whether she could discern the exact type of alcohol (moderately difficult under present conditions) as well as the approximate amount (impossible but an entertaining challenge) in her drink and she wondered why that one girl in the back kept giving her dirty looks and she thought about getting pushed up against the wall of the apartment and violently fucked in front of everyone else at the party and she thought about how she owed her mother a month's worth of phone calls and she thought about how exactly they would get back to the dorm when the campus shuttle stopped running at midnight and she thought about where precisely the stairs were to the second floor of the house, the kind of stairs that one might be led up by a thick indifferent college boy before he pinned her to a mattress beneath his sticky shuddering torso. Such things played in her mind.

She sat down in a big armchair and felt the regret of all partygoers who squander their momentum by surrendering to a too-comfortable seat. There were people on a couch next to her, and she tried to signal vague greetings to them, but the chair was in her way, enveloping her as she settled into it until it occluded her peripheral vision. She felt claustrophobic and tired and worried that everyone was staring at her and judging her for relaxing at a party, though most of the attendees were too preoccupied with their own social awkwardness. Alice judged herself all the same:

It was ridiculous to sit so early in the night, as though admitting defeat, surrendering all hope of successful social interaction. But after barely ninety seconds of sitting, she knew bolting back up again risked making her look weird, or weirder, and the people seated on the couch would definitely notice. So she took out her cell phone as theatrically as she could manage and paged through it with a great show of concentration. Corn-fed had liked the photo she'd posted of herself in her cat costume but not the one of her and Clara taken fifteen minutes later. This was unfortunate. It would be a pity if he made a move, if he were to graduate from subtle digital flirtation to messaging her late at night, because Alice could not fathom saying no.

Clara rescued Alice then by crying out her name in a whiny sing-song white-girl voice, which made Alice flush with relief for this excuse to escape the chair and guilt for having been daydreaming about the corn-fed boy. Clara said she wanted Alice to meet someone and led her roughly away by the wrist, and Alice allowed herself to be dragged; she had been the girl being pulled through a party by a more confident peer many times in her life. She was worried about Clara and worried that the person she was about to meet could become the object of Clara's next bout of gasping sobs. Alice was already thinking through the various techniques she might use to guide Clara to the sweet spot of making out, or perhaps getting fingered, but of not sleeping with whoever this guy was. To Alice's relief, unless it was disappointment, Clara was tipsy but not wasted and kept herself composed. Alice's expectation had been that Clara would party like she had something to prove. Then they were out back after all and she was meeting the boy.

He was tall but skinny and his wrists looked thinner than Alice's. He had long dark brown hair and wore a leather vest over a white T-shirt, along with a number of black leather bracelets with little metallic charms; perhaps he was hoping to distract from those wrists, but he succeeded only in calling attention to them. He was dark-eyed and had a certain attractive wolfish quality but he also looked to Alice something like a junior high school student, and she decided quickly that she wasn't a fan of his face. He was smoking a cigarette like someone who wanted other people to see that he was smoking a cigarette, and he extended her hand to her with an exaggerated diffidence. She knew before she was told that he was an actor and found him annoying before he opened his mouth.

"This is Evan," Clara was saying. The giggle that accompanied her introduction sounded no more organic than the way Evan was smoking his cigarette and for a moment Alice felt consumed by artificiality, by the weight of other people's performances. But it occurred to her that she was herself wearing a literal costume on a night devoted to pretending to be other things, and she forgave them both.

"What's your story?" he said, and she enjoyed a brief fantasy of rolling her eyes at his affectation and wandering away. Instead she dutifully introduced herself. He was a sophomore, still undeclared, and somehow from New Hampshire. She asked how someone from New Hampshire ended up at Oklahoma University and he stammered out a few words about football; this seemed incongruous given his personal style. But she liked it, the stammering, the awkward embarrassment, and decided that he was at his best when he was on his back foot. She helped him recover by asking him what his costume was.

"Jim Morrison," he said. His eyes danced and she realized that he was daring her to ask who that was. She knew she should be annoyed but he was growing on her; she studied his features for some subtle cuteness but could not find it, seeing only the plain and anxious face of a boy who was trying hard to appear unconcerned. Still, she could grow to like any face, if she put her mind to it. The question was whether he would prove worthy of the effort. First, though, the matter at hand: There was no way she was going to give him the satisfaction.

"*L.A. Woman* era, I take it," she said. Her father was precisely the kind of father who taught his indifferent daughter about The Doors.

He cocked his eyebrow at her, and again she pondered how much affectation she was willing to excuse. She took another pull of punch and Clara reminded her of her presence.

"Oooooh," she said, "looks like you met your match," and Evan raised his Solo cup in a mock salute, and Alice gratefully gave Clara the floor. Alice admired Clara's people skills, her ability to act as a social lubricant, and once again thanked whatever algorithm had placed them together. A few more minutes of uncomfortable conversation and Alice and Clara retreated for more drinks. Evan was left taking another long drag on his cigarette, for an audience of no one.

"Well?" asked Clara as she poured too much vodka into Alice's cup. Someone was loudly asking if anyone there had any shrooms. Predictably the answer was no.

"Well he's a poseur," said Alice, "but he's kind of endearing."

She poured root beer into the cup and took a sip. She did another self-sobriety test and felt well enough. She figured that as long as the thoughts were still pouring into her brain she couldn't be that far gone. And they were pouring. Her mind had for now lost its fixation on sex and was instead obsessing over whether or not the boy had in fact been dressed in a particularly *L.A. Woman* style, whether there really was any such thing as an *L.A. Woman* style, and whether Alice would have been able to identify it if she saw it.

"So are you gonna go for it?" asked Clara.

"Who, me? I thought he was for you."

"Nope," said Clara. "I don't date white men."

A rule that couldn't have been more than about forty-five minutes old, based on past conversations, but Alice had gotten used to such pronouncements from Clara. More pressing was how she felt about Clara "giving" Evan to her. Alice knew that Clara really did want her to be happy. She also knew that Clara would only try to set her up with someone Clara felt wasn't good enough for her own personal use.

"He's gross," said Alice. "He doesn't know how to be himself."

"It's Halloween, my dear!" said Clara. "No one's supposed to be themselves." She was gulping down enough vodka and cranberry to reignite Alice's concerns even as she rewarded Clara's comment with a sincere laugh.

"I'm off to flirt," she said, and drew Alice in for a quick kiss on the cheek. "I love you."

Off she went. Alice's motherly instincts were still active, but she told herself that Clara was far more likely to remain in control that night than she was herself. She was pleasantly buzzed and could see as though on a highway sign the limits of her tolerance approaching; if she killed the drink in her hands and poured another, she would be crossing the border between attractive drunk to look-at-that-mess drunk. Mess drunk would either result in Clara taking care of her or Clara not taking care of her. If the former, Clara would resent her for it; if the latter, Alice would resent Clara. Also, mess drunk meant figuring out how to get home without decorating an Uber with her vomit or getting passed around by frat guys. No. This drink was to nurse, not to pound.

Or it would have been if she could bear to keep thinking. She wanted to blunt the impact of her thoughts, which multiplied incessantly, pinballing against each other and the walls of her mind, spooling out in fractal patterns that were totally predictable and yet surprised her nonetheless, like watching the slow progression of a terminal disease in a loved one's body and still feeling shocked when they die. She was frowning, a war playing out between her desire to pummel her brain with alcohol and her fear of rape, when she noticed a boy advancing on her in that typical unfortunate way. She pretended not to see him and ducked through the back door.

Within moments a joint was pressed between her lips and she was inhaling lustily. Some dim part of her wiser mind sounded the alarm that this the thing she needed least, that the thoughts had already been threatening to outrun the dulling effects of alcohol, and that to encourage them now was to ensure unhappiness to come. But Clara was off doing her own thing and Alice dreaded another awkward conversation and as ever smoking weed presented the perfect social conditions, a circle of amiable someones concentrating on something other than you and who were used to people going suddenly and deeply silent. Alice chuckled at jokes she couldn't really hear and made guttural assenting sounds when the girl next to her complained about the party, and she didn't even mind that the guy who had brought the weed was trying so hard to maintain flirtatious eye contact. At some point she arrived at the stage where she could no longer gauge where the alcohol ended and the weed began, and she wandered away, no doubt exiting some half-conversation abruptly.

She found her way to Evan. His looks annoyed her even more but his face was newly inviting to a stumbling, disoriented Alice. And while he was still standing in an artificial pose, sucking down another cigarette with entirely too much effort, he seemed more relaxed than before, the steady war of attrition between alcohol and ego nearing its inevitable end. Evan saw Alice, grinned, then slunk back into artificial diffidence. It was endearing this time.

"What's up, Jim?" she said.

"The beauty of that joke is that if you actually did forget my name it's the perfect cover," he said.

"Evan," she said, and lurched. She noticed him noticing her stumble and was unsure of how to feel about it. "You know those things will kill you."

"I know," he said, taking a last drag. "I'd love to say something cool about not caring if I live or die, but I'm applying for summer internships already and that's a little too much hypocrisy even for me."

She laughed away her last bit of resistance to him, not sexual or romantic but simply as a person.

"So he has a little self-knowledge," she said.

"A little."

They chatted for a long while. Occasionally someone would join them. Alice was aware that she was clinging to Evan long enough for it to become a thing, but to wander back out into the minefield of strangers seemed like an impossible task. She was determined not to join the ranks of the other partygoers sitting alone, nursing beers, shy outcasts looking like shy outcasts, whatever pretenses they'd brought along. Besides, Evan more than alcohol seemed to be keeping the parade of Alice's unwanted thoughts at bay. Before she knew it an hour had passed, and every time a noncombatant came back into their orbit she was thankful, for she and Evan had run out of things to talk about but were conspicuously not flirting. In time, though, rescues became scarce. No one wanted to go near them, whether to avoid intruding on their moment or to avoid being sucked into their discomfort. It wasn't awkward enough to drive Alice away, but she was annoyed that Evan hadn't made a move; she wasn't sure she would respond in kind, wasn't sure she even wanted it to happen, but it would add a dose of clarity to an evening that had started out weird and gotten weirder. Alice wanted desperately for Clara to reappear, and right at that moment she did.

With relief she stumbled away from Evan and over to Clara, grasping at her hand. Clara looked at her with warmth but with obvious concern. Alice was hurt that Clara was not inspired to embrace her.

"Oh, boy," she said. "Having fun?"

"I'm fine," said Alice, her relief now annoyance. "I'm barely drunk."

"Okay," said Clara. "I'm heading home."

"Oh, are you?" said Alice. "Whose home?"

Clara's laugh was tired. Her usual conspiratorial attitude had abandoned her. Alice felt very alone.

"Our home. No boys tonight, sweetie."

Alice was briefly moved to express mock sympathy but realized it would not be appreciated. Clara stroked Alice's hair.

"I think you should come with me."

There was a brief struggle in Alice's mind. She knew Clara was right, and bed sounded inviting. But suddenly and powerfully Alice felt, too that Clara was patronizing her, and it filled her with defiance and suspicion.

"I'm talking to Evan," she said.

"You don't like Evan."

"He's growing on me."

Clara sighed, and again Alice found herself grappling with dark thoughts about Clara's motives. She shook off her suspicion, for the time being, but not her defiance.

"I'm getting an Uber," said Clara, pulling up her phone. "How are you getting back?"

"I'll figure it out."

"It'll be here in six minutes. I'm going to wait in the front yard. Come out before then if you want a ride."

Alice felt nothing upon hearing this ultimatum. Before Clara turned to go, however, she grabbed Alice's wrist and embraced her. Alice hugged her back.

"Be careful," she said.

Her defiance exhausted, Alice's paranoid fantasies seized their moment, rallied, and attacked. New narratives spooled out for her about why Clara should have acted the way she did. The clock on Alice's phone told her that Clara would be gone in four minutes. She thought about how she would never have forced Clara to make the same choice, how she would have stayed with her no matter what, how if Clara had wanted to stay she would have waited all night for her. Her sense of betrayal grew. She was so distracted by watching it grow that only two minutes remained by the time it flowered. She couldn't bear to watch those two minutes tick down, was desperate to arrest her thinking, so she stumbled back to Evan, laying her hand on his hip, breaking all the unspoken rules their exchange had thus far obeyed.

"Whoa," he said, steadying her. His face annoyed her more than ever.

"Take me upstairs," she breathed, letting her fingers brush against the skin just above the waistline of his pants.

"What's upstairs?"

She struggled to think of a response. Rather than collapse she leaned closer and drew his hand to her breast.

"Whatever you want," she said, vaguely aware of how sad she sounded.

"Oh, hey, haha," he said, pulling back from her. "I think you're pretty drunk."

She sighed in aggravation. "I'm fine. Come take what you want."

"I don't want anything that you wouldn't give me when you were sober," he said. It sounded sincere, to Alice, and fairly noble, but like everything Evan said it sounded rehearsed, and her sense of defiance flared up anew.

"Well there's another boy somewhere who wants to fuck me," she said, and turned as if to go, a little more slowly than she would have done if she had any intention of leaving.

"That's not a good idea either," Evan said. "Look, this party's a drag, want to go to the diner and eat?" This seemed as though it might be the real Evan speaking, dropping whatever was left of the pose he had adopted for the evening. Was his pretention a Halloween-only sort of thing or was it his usual mode? Alice made a mental note to get back to this question in the light of day.

"I have to pee," she said. "Where's your car?"

"Out front," he said, but looked at her with concern. "Can I walk you to the bathroom?"

"I'm fine," she snapped. "Out front in ten." She stumbled off before he could say more.

She wended her way through the party. Several boys eyed her hungrily as she passed, but she was moving with precision, driven to greater self-control by her sense of danger. The stairs were a challenge, but soon she was standing in line outside of the bathroom. A couple dressed in matching Frankenstein and Bride costumes were snorting coke in the hallway, sitting with their backs to a locked bedroom door—a little bold, but she reminded herself that it was almost 2:00 a.m. She was deeply annoyed to find that the friends of the crying girl ahead of her had decided that the bathroom was the right place to calm her down, but before too long they stumbled out and Alice stumbled in. She was confronted with the mirror and the thoughts took her completely.

Her cat makeup had smeared worse than ever, somehow, no longer looking playful but like a serious mess, and Alice blamed Clara without knowing why. The cleavage she had felt so proud of now looked despondent and unimpressive, a record of a young woman trying to be something she wasn't, and she wondered where she could find a shirt to throw on top. She tried to think through what she wanted from Evan; typically she knew right away if she liked someone, but she couldn't decide if she wanted him to take her violently in the parking lot of the diner or to give her his number and drop her straight off at home or to stay up with her until the sun rose talking about the future. She studied every pore of her face and found only imperfection. Someone knocked in annoyance on the bathroom door, but rather than speed her progress, it caused her to withdraw further inside herself in fright. It was a battle to get down onto the toilet. She peed and while she did so she cooked up a thousand scenarios, all the times Clara may have conspired against her. She opened Instagram on her phone and messaged the corn-fed boy:

"hey"

She had banana walnut pancakes and three glasses of water. Evan had eggs and sausage. They had arrived at that pleasant point in the evening where their dying buzz and deepening exhaustion drained whatever awkwardness remained between them. Alice joked and laughed and Evan dutifully chuckled along, seeming entirely spent, until the check came. Alice waited to see if he would grab it himself, decided she didn't want him to, and lurched to throw some cash down before he could say anything. He drove her to her dorm and sat with the engine running. Her feelings about him were no clearer than they had been all night, but she spent a long while thinking how she had gotten dressed up that night expecting some sort of intimacy from some self-centered boy or other. No action from Evan was forthcoming, so she placed her hand on his knee.

He leaned in and gave her a kiss, exactly the kiss she had wanted. He didn't kiss like a skinny try-hard but like a man who was hungry but composed, gripping her head with just a little too much force, too much but just right. She bit his lower lip and then withdrew, one last little touch she hoped he found sexy. He grinned and ran his hand through his hair, pushing it back over his ear, finally unpretentious and unguarded. For a moment everything was perfect.

"So you want to drive someplace quiet and I'll pipe you down?" he said, and if that wasn't bad enough his voice cracked while he said it. Alice knew it was time to stop humoring him and she gave him a glance that she hoped was withering.

"You were doing so good," she said. He stammered and apologized, which did more to evaporate the effect of the kiss than did his failed invitation.

"Shhh," she said, unzipping his pants. She worked her hand unhurriedly up and down, gradually adding more pressure as she had learned to, listening to him gasp. Cars puttered past from time to time, but she was unconcerned, and she worked diligently until she heard the telltale half-moan. She wiped her hands on a McDonald's bag from the floor of the car, then got out without saying goodnight.

Clara lay sleeping in her bed in their room. To Alice in that moment she looked like a slumbering angel; she realized that this was exactly the kind of thing her mother would say, that a sleeping person looked like an angel, but she was unconcerned with such thoughts in that tender light. With incredible delicacy she reached down to brush away a single lock of Clara's dark hair. She felt the love of true friendship, and as she stared at Clara she also felt that she was looking at her enemy, someone who was conspiring to harm her at all times, a shadowy figure who was working in the background to marginalize Alice and thwart her plans and cause her pain. Climbing into bed, lying there waiting to pass out, Alice knew that she would have to hurt Clara first.

Three

Alice's mother hummed when she was worried, and she had been doing it all day. Alice bummed a ride home from a sweet and slight gay boy she'd befriended in one of her classes. Her father kept insisting via text message that he should come get her, but she had shrugged him off, first with a curt text back and then with silence. She didn't want him to see her room, and she was afraid of allowing any further interaction between her parents and Clara, though they had gotten on so well the one time they met. So Alice lied and told her parents that her friend lived a town over, when in fact he lived a 45-minute drive away, and she had paid for half a tank of gas with her dwindling savings.

Now she was picking through underwear at a TJ Maxx with her mother, who kept hovering near Alice and making pointless small talk. Alice had made the mistake of telling her that she was failing a class, compelled by some sort of quasi-religious guilt over falling behind while her father spent every spare cent on her education. Her mother seemed more concerned with her weight loss, running her hand down Alice's side several times to feel her ribs. It figured that she would worry; Alice's fitness goals were just about the only thing that had gone right in her first semester at ou.

Still, Thanksgiving break was here and Alice was glad. She and Clara had been fighting incessantly, in their usual style of intense intimacy interspersed with passive aggression and flares of recrimination. Clara was spending more and more time with others, sometimes bringing Alice along, sometimes inviting her while making it clear she wasn't really wanted, sometimes giggling into her cellphone while getting ready to go out without saying a word to Alice at all. And the next day the two of them would shuffle off groggily to the dining hall and gorge on waffles and laugh and joke like nothing had happened.

But the balance between intimacy and conflict was skewing toward the latter mode. For one thing, Clara kept rearranging the items in Alice's shower caddie. It was subtle, and Alice found that Clara had a sixth sense about not doing it when Alice was expecting it—she had stuck a piece of hidden tape across the bottoms of her conditioner and her body wash to see if they were disturbed, but came home to find it intact, a sign of Clara's dedication to deception. Alice had taken to obsessively photographing the caddie whenever she left the apartment alone and then again upon her return, but she found that she struggled to examine the evidence effectively—the colors danced and the lines refused to focus and she could never quite perceive the differences in the photos, if any, and thus proof eluded her. "No smoking gun yet" she had scribbled in one of her many secret notebooks, on a page deep in the middle so no one would find it, and then thought for an hour about how the smoke from a gun must smell.

In class she was suffering, not failing but limping to Cs, unable to concentrate, but where it came to other endeavors, her attention had honed down to a razor acuity. However elusive proof had remained, Alice felt no shortage of attention when it came to collecting evidence of Clara's slowly-gathering betrayal. She had nothing but attention.

But Clara was gone, now, off to Tulsa to see her family. Alice was alone with her parents and so had the opportunity to be reminded of the freedom she had left behind. Alice had never been much of a problem child, despite her casual dabbling in sex and drugs, but she found the ever-present eye of her mother to be a painful constraint the minute she walked in the door. She had hoped for a break from Clara's constant surveillance but now found two pairs of eyes boring into her instead of one. Her father would never say anything to bother her, she knew, but she also knew that her mother was daily regaling him with her list of worries over Alice's wellbeing, education, and morals. Now she was finding that their shopping trip taken to help expand Alice's collection of underwear could not possibly result in her actually buying any, as she feared the inferences her mother might draw from Alice's selecting any given pair. To Alice's considerable relief her mother chalked up her demurrals to frugality.

She was to see her Sadie the next day. Sadie's brief electronic interactions had become something of an oasis for Alice, even as she was forced to trudge through the daily complaints about the boys she liked who did not like her back, who liked her back too much, or who otherwise failed to meet her exacting standards. Sadie had reported that she too had lost weight, and she had cried while catching up with Alice many times, but she always insisted she loved college, USC, and Los Angeles. Alice's motherhen instincts had been on standby for months and she was eager to care for someone again.

But first she had to manage her mother, who had now dragged her to a variety store that her father referred to as "the Christmas store" twelve months out of the year. Their ritual was unvarying: they would hunt exhaustively through every aisle, her mother would remark on what a great deal every last item in the store was, and they would buy nothing. Alice dipped deep into her well of patient and kind regard, not just for her mother but for everyone, and she was impeccably cordial throughout the ordeal. When they got home, though, Alice asked if she might please take her mother's car out for a drive, a request that was granted at once.

She drove out to a big empty space she knew. "Big empty space in Oklahoma" might sound almost romantic, but Alice's spot was only dirty, the red-brown dirt she had gazed out on one drive after another throughout her childhood. There was nothing built here, but also nothing wild. Even the weeds poking out between the patches of concrete hadn't made much of an effort. An abandoned car sat rusting a ways off; Alice avoided it, for fear of something leaping out at her. She thought she saw hypodermic needles in a sickly patch of flax-colored grass and there was no shade from the November sun. And yet the landscape gave her what she wanted, which was a contrast from her environment at school.

It was just an empty space, a place where her troubled thoughts could vanish off into the horizon. She called it Big Flat. The OU campus was too perfect, the quads too manicured, the brown-red buildings too grand. There was a paper doll quality to the place, and certainly to the people there. Alice had lost count of the number of girls who had told her, contemptuously, that some other girl was lying about having Chickasaw heritage; sometimes they were complaining about each other. There were blonde girls with big tits who went to football games and tried to get on ESPN's cameras and there were thick Black guys with farm-raised bodies and thin sweaty dudes who played with drones and men who referred to everyone as "hoss." Old white-haired professors shuffled across the campus lawns while the young, cool, strapping professors chatted at high volume with every passing student, flirting right up to the line, never stepping over it under their own power but always ready to be pulled across by the lightest touch. On gamedays the whole region swelled with drunkards, gamblers, and sports reporters who wouldn't have minded finding the right undergraduate to bring back to the hotel. There were the night shuttles that took drunk girls safely home to the dorms, and there were the male students who rode them to offer those students a helping hand back up to their rooms and into their beds.

Alice would have liked to see it all as the great human pageant she had imagined when she dreamed of college back in high school, but lately all she saw were too many vectors of deception. She was fond of imagining that if she had gotten into one of the elite little New England colleges of her dreams, everything would have been different, she would have been popular and an academic star and in love, a lie transparent even to her but one she permitted herself to tell.

So now she was here, among the dirt and trash. She could have found a more pleasant landscape, could conceivably have made it to Robbers Cave if she had really wanted to. But she didn't want to. She wanted to be out in the empty space of this ugly lot, where the rusty earth receded away from her faster than her mind could follow. Her thoughts had taken to multiplying and doubling back on themselves so relentlessly that she had ceased attempting to direct their traffic; in class they would either gravitate toward the professor and the material sufficiently that she might pass the upcoming test, or they would not. Her horniness had become constant and relentless, and only the thin shield of her shyness prevented her from dragging the next moderately attractive classmate into a bathroom stall. Out here, though, she was steady and her mind quiet, as if in this grubby loneliness she had found something worthy of her fixation. For once her intent and her attention were the same. She sat on the hood of her car and let the flow of thoughts that had no form and no direction speed their way to that distant line, not the perfect expanse of the Oklahoma plains but the unbothered ugliness of this discarded place. She felt exhausted and content. Then she drove home.

A strained afternoon followed with her father, who laughed when he called her skinny but stepped his weight from one foot to another while he did so, always a sign that he was anxious. Alice killed the time and the potential for conversation by watching several hours of television about renovating houses. Then she arrived an hour early to the diner parking lot, a place where she had whiled away many hours as a teenager. Now there was no relaxation to be had, only worry, and she wore away her fingernails with her teeth until they were raw and bleeding.

Then there she was, Sadie, her beloved Sadie. They swept each other up in a hug. The old love was there, immediately, and just as immediately Alice knew that some of their decade-old ease was gone. Sadie groped Alice's ribs theatrically, and for the hundredth time Alice chuckled out some weak explanation about cutting out carbs. It took her awhile to reorient herself to Sadie's human face; she had become too accustomed to the flat artificiality of video calls. She was beautiful, as she always was, but her face was ringed with the sadness of a person who had grown tired of faking smiles. They got their usual booth and Alice robotically ordered Sadie's chicken fingers and her own cheese fries, though the thought of eating sickened her. She played with her food while Sadie talked.

"I'm 70 percent sure I'm dropping out," said Sadie, who went on to recount everything wrong with USC, and LA, and college in general. Her first instinct, she said, was to join Alice at OU. Alice told her that this sounded more like transferring than dropping out, but she knew Sadie liked the grandiosity of the more dramatic verb. She grappled internally with the fact that she loved and missed Sadie, that she wished they could spend more time together, and that she absolutely did not want to go to the same college as she did. She wanted to feel Sadie's light, but she did not want her own to be dimmed in its presence. For the fortieth time she leaned over to see if anyone had stolen her car.

It turned out that LA was superficial, or perhaps only USC was. It turned out that the men there were effeminate and insufficiently commanding, except for when they tried to pressure her into sex, which they did constantly. It turned out that her female friends were fake, except when they were clinging and suffocating. Alice nodded along while inside her heart flipflopped at every mention of Sadie's many new friends, however annoying Sadie found them. It was all vintage Sadie, and true to form she had no real intention of transferring, nor any notion of what she might do outside of school beyond a vague desire to work in fashion. Sadie had always exaggerated and overreacted and made plans in which she truly believed and that despite that sincerity would never be acted upon; and Alice had always assented, always amplified, always believed, without skepticism or judgment. And here in the same diner where they'd done it all before, Alice knew that this was her mission, her mission from God, to believe this person, right here, right now, this person she had no reason to believe. It felt like a sacred calling and the weight of that responsibility did not feel like weight at all but like sacred electricity that filled her body, the booth, the diner, the world. Her car was still there.

"I need to go to the bathroom," said Sadie, sounding unsure.

"Then just go," said Alice. But Sadie hovered, looking conflicted, studying the table. When she looked up she looked up into Alice's eyes, smiling, grasping her wrist and tugging her along to the bathroom.

It was, as it always had been, impeccably clean. Sadie locked the door.

"What are, uh, what are we doing?" asked Alice.

Sadie dug into her bag for a small pink compact. She opened it on the ledge of the sink. Inside, opposite its little mirror, was a compartment filled with cocaine.

Alice forced herself to be arrested by the inherent drama of the moment. She had dreamed often of her first time snorting cocaine, and while she had many fantasies about how it might go down (with a celebrity at a club, on a drunken fuck weekend with a lover, in Venice or some other vaguely exotic place), none of them involved the bathroom of the diner in her hometown.

But she could see Sadie about to speak and could detect defensive feelings forming on Sadie's face, and then she could think of nothing she needed to avoid more than hearing what Sadie had to say. She had to silence her, to deny this moment, this moment when the person who trusted her the most felt compelled to share a bevy of justifications that Alice didn't need to hear. So she did the only thing that came to mind and plunged her head down to the compact and, with no lines cut and only her bare nostril, snorted some coke.

She felt woozy as she rose, but also pretty sure this was because of the speed with which she had jerked her head down and back up. A little powder tumbled from her nose. She was trying to sort out if she was already high when she noted that Sadie was looking at her with real concern.

"That's not the way you do it, silly," she said, grasping Alice's arm with a gentle touch and steadying her.

"Then cut them up," said Alice, sniffling. "Cut 'em up."

And Sadie did, and they both did two lines, then floated back to their table. Alice's cheese fries were cold but she started to eat them, three or four at a time. Sadie's sadness had lifted. Alice's car was still there every time she checked, once, twice, a dozen times. They ordered milkshakes to prolong the night, stole back into the bathroom, then parted with untroubled and sincere hugs, tears that were real tears.

Alice drove back to her childhood home, focused and intent, scanning everywhere for the thieves that would steal into her room at night, and when she pressed the accelerator it was the thrum of life itself, the strident pulse of one who would never die.

Four

There was no picture online of the person at ou's counseling center whom Alice had been instructed to see. This fact had vexed Alice since she received her marching orders from the administration. It was now more than a month into her second semester at ou. Her sagging fall grades had given way to sterling performance in the spring, as there was now always time, always time to read and to study and to think. Alice was pleased to find that she could function perfectly on four hours of sleep a night, and while her many emailed requests that the library remain open twenty-four hours had thus far gone unreturned, she found that she could power her way across campus with her earbuds in until it reopened at 7:30 a.m., and by the time they unlocked the door for her she would in any case have whittled her thoughts down to the purest and sharpest expression of whatever it was she had felt compelled to learn. Her social calendar was getting emptier and emptier in parallel with her newfound acuity, and after a month of crawling into the corn-fed boy's cramped twin bed late at night even he no longer returned her texts. So she studied, and when her RA summoned her to a strained meeting at the residential life department she had received the subpoena with clinical distance.

When she was informed by Res Life that she would be required to undergo an evaluation, she naturally set about researching the Counseling Center. She read the pamphlet they had pressed into her hands as avidly as a rabbinical student pondering the Talmud. Her professor called this "reading against the grain," and she took to the process immediately, finding the deeper meanings and hidden valences others couldn't see. The pamphlet was crawling with

Straussian material, symbols laden with meanings she knew she could decode if she could only find the thread. She took to their website to do just that, but always ran aground when she found the space where the headshot of the woman she was meant to meet ought to have been. The sickly gray placeholder-thumbnail sapped Alice's energy every time she navigated to the page. It couldn't be coincidence.

She wore a hoodie over a thick T-shirt and her sports bra but she still shivered as she sat in the waiting room. She was twenty pounds lighter than the day she first arrived on campus and she wasn't overweight then. She drew her legs up and hugged her knees, snaking her right arm up inside her sweatshirt to press at her spot, the one just below her left armpit. She felt the spongey cyst that had developed there and grinned a tight grin at the little spike of pain. She fought down the urge to use her earbuds; she was in the house of liars and she needed all of her senses.

When they called her name she rose calmly and walked up to the desk calmly and nodded her head calmly when they sent her down the hall, and when she looked inside the little office at the end of the hall to find a mousy South Asian woman with kind eyes she shook the counselor's hand, no problem. Alice sat on a comfortable armchair and despite the sense that she might sink so far into it that she might never emerge, she felt more level than she had in weeks.

As the counselor took her own chair behind her desk, Alice saw how small she was without the benefit of her tall heels. She was dressed conservatively but the pink frames of her glasses were dotted with little red hearts.

"Before we begin, Alice, I want you to understand that I am not here to evaluate or diagnose you today, and this is not a disciplinary hearing," the counselor said. The office was artfully designed: metal shelves groaned with yellowing old journals, a large mahogany desk in the corner with no visible computer, and various bric-a-brac no doubt designed to induce comfort—one of those toys with the metal balls that clacked together, origami giraffes and unicorns, *The Big Book of Little Blessings* on a side table. The analog wall clock caught Alice's eye; the time it displayed was a full twelve minutes ahead. She rearranged herself in her quicksand seat and, conscious that the doctor had said something, nodded her head.

"So," said the doctor, "I understand you've had a talk with the people in Residential Life."

"Yeah," said Alice. Her head was hurting. It hadn't been hurting a minute ago.

"Do you understand why we're having this dialogue?"

Alice knew, of course, that Clara must have complained, but the people with Res Life had refused to name names.

"My roommate isn't happy. I guess. I guess my roommate isn't too happy. Too, too happy. I don't know. She's not happy. Too-too happy."

The doctor scribbled a note. Alice imagined a satellite scouring her with its merciless beams.

"Today we're not here to talk about those specifics," said the doctor, chipper. "The important point is that Res Life is concerned that you're not finding school easy."

Alice would have been the first to admit that her initial semester had been rough, but over the past couple months she had found school easier than it ever had been before. "Um, I'm happy," she said, and wondered if that were true.

"But you're having trouble adjusting," said the doctor, eyes unwavering beneath those glasses, enunciating so crisply it hurt.

It was clear that there was a right answer. Alice sought it in the carpet and the ceiling and in the hum of the air conditioning. "Yes," she said. "Trouble adjusting." She couldn't tell if she was whispering. The doctor looked pleased, so it was probably all right.

"You've been struggling in class, I take it." The woman shuffled her clipboard to glance at her iPhone.

"No," said Alice. "I'm acing everything now."

"It's okay," said the doctor, irritated by something on her screen. "Here there's no need for false courage."

"Okay," said Alice. "Struggling in class."

The doctor awarded her another point. She wrote her next note in her book with swirling and crisp strokes.

"It's not unusual at all," she said. "And stress does funny things."

Not having been asked a question, Alice only nodded.

"So tell me about your anxieties lately," said the doctor.

"My anxieties," said Alice. She had nothing but anxieties, anxieties about everything, anxieties about what lay behind every bush, anxieties about the boys she hooked up with and what they might be hiding in their pockets, anxieties about her father's lungs and her mother's lymph nodes, anxieties about the fact that her heart beat so fast at night while she lay in bed not sleeping. Her world was anxiety, and around every corner lay death, ruin, ridicule.

"Have you ever been evaluated by a psychiatrist before, Alice?"

"No," said Alice.

"Well, I am a licensed clinical social worker, but I don't want to play that role today," said the doctor. "I want you to tell me: if a friend, a close friend, asked you what you think about, the kind of things you fixate on, what's running through your mind, now or at any time . . . what would you tell that friend?"

The counselor pumped the plunger on her pen three times, drawing the tip in and out. Alice swam through what the doctor had just said, searching it for all of its possible valences, hoping to take it apart schematically, quantitatively, like a robot. Instead she felt very alone and very exposed and so she simply told the truth, afraid of how a lie might ring false in that sterile office.

"I go up and down," she said. "I am beset with monsters. My roommate seeks to dominate me, she places rice into my food, the rice expands in my belly in the night and it threatens me, it threatens my heart, I sleep with a boy named Craig from the next dorm over and he holds himself inside of me after he comes so that he can imprint his DNA onto mine. I can read the writing behind the writing in my favorite class, the professor is warning me of dreadful things to come. I am so vulnerable, so alone and subject to every passing person's thoughts. I fear my own power. I fear my own blood will pour out of my eyes and drown the people I pass in the halls and it will mix with their own blood. I feel I am allergic to wind and the milk in the dining hall tastes like sawdust." She went silent for a beat, then turned her head so that her left eye looked directly into the hood of her sweatshirt. She chuckled into the fabric.

The doctor clicked her pen twice, four times, eight, twelve times more, with no overt sign of concern, rock-steady except that she pushed back from her desk, leaned forward ever so slightly in her chair, farther, farther. She fished a page out of her desk drawer.

"Yes," said the doctor. "You're very tired."

She was leaning so far forward Alice was afraid she might topple and injure herself. She started leaning toward the doctor herself in hopes of catching her before she cracked her nose.

"Very tired," the doctor said, then pressed the paper into Alice's hand. "But this will tell you what you need to know."

Twenty minutes later Alice was walking back to her dorm. In her pocket was a prescription for Klonopin. In her hand she clutched the paper. It was a brochure. On it a model in a stock photo smiled, a beatific and calm smile, the smile of a child, the smile of someone who wasn't there. Beneath her ran the words, "Dealing with Stress."

Five

Alice and Clara ambled across campus, headed to no particular destination. Clara wasn't due to move her things out until the following afternoon, but when she asked Alice to take a walk with her Alice understood that it was their last ride.

The fighting had died down. Clara let Alice know that she would be living in a friend's off-campus apartment for the remainder of the semester—"off the books," as she put it, presumably to reassure Alice that there would be no more problems with Res Life. With her trademark desire to find an edge in all things, Clara mentioned how she had found an apartment for next year, too, calling it a "head start" on off-campus life. Her announcement sucked all the tension out of their room, leaving behind only sadness. In the weeks previous, Alice had come to understand that Clara was her enemy, a chaos agent sent to slow Alice's ascent toward becoming what she was meant to become. But when Clara broke the news, Alice still went to the dorm's shared bathroom, turned on the shower, and sobbed in the stall.

They walked in unusual silence and in an unseasonable chill. Alice was afraid to say anything; she had spent many long nights speaking incessantly to Clara, recounting all of her thoughts, faster and faster as the hours wore by. She knew that this was aggravating to Clara, knew that she was gradually eroding every remaining ounce of affection Clara still bore for her, and she hated doing it, but found she could not stop, indeed found that her very concern for not overwhelming Clara compelled her to speak faster and more recklessly, compelled her to overwrite every inane thing she said with something new. Clara exhibited great patience at first, and would in most cases resort to a polite, "Honey, I have to study," but Alice was relentless and eventually Clara had taken to putting in her earbuds without a word.

Campus was oddly quiet too. Perhaps the students were staying indoors due to the chill, alien in an Oklahoma April. Alice didn't feel the temperature. She felt only an all-over buzzing, a constant tingling that ran all over her skin, racing up one arm, across the back of her neck, and down the other. It rose when it wanted to and it was not unpleasant, but it contributed to the sense that everything in and around Alice was accelerating all the time. Clara dug her hands into her ou windbreaker.

They came to the lion fountain at the north end of campus. Behind it stood one of the school's grand brick buildings, built in a style Alice had come to see as dishonest for reasons she could not articulate. The stone lions spit into the fountain, mocking her. Alice fingered a penny in the pocket of her jeans, pondering a wish. No, she was too exposed here. Too self-conscious. She took a seat on a bench, and Clara followed her.

"It's close enough that I can take a shuttle," said Clara. She sounded calm but was leaning forward on the bench as though ready to bolt. The finality of their parting struck Alice for the first time. She had told herself none of it was a big deal; the semester would be over in a month, and hardly anybody kept living with their freshman roommate anyway. But Alice had few other friends at ou, if she had any, and a month alone in the dorm would only give way to three more years of sadness, she was sure, and then to a life lived right here in the buzzy anxious tingling she could not escape.

"Won't you be lonely?" said Alice. It sounded pathetic coming from her in that moment, but she had said it now, and could only sit with it.

"I actually think I have people lined up for the other two rooms," said Clara. "One to move in come June, and one in August." This was obviously a dodge, but it was a merciful one, given how it avoided taking account of the unmistakable panic in Alice's words. But Clara seemed to know she couldn't leave it at that.

"It just got hard between us, sweetie," she said, and let the sentence linger. "It just gets hard, sometimes, even between people who care about each other."

She reached over and squeezed Alice's hand. Alice knew, with the kind of deep knowing available only to a fractured mind, that Clara would delicately but purposefully drift out of Alice's life for good once they were physically separated.

"You're leaving me," Alice said. "Because you're afraid of my light."

Clara looked down at her shoes with pursed lips.

"Let's walk," she said, and so they did, vaguely in the direction of their dorm. Undergraduates in fifty-dollar ou-branded hooded sweatshirts filed past, hurrying to classes or to the library or to find a quiet place to smoke up. Alice had spent the first few months of college thinking of every face on campus as that of a friend she had yet to meet, but lately they all seemed dark, haunted, and inscrutable. Alice had found herself with no sex partner in recent weeks and it left her feeling cranky and untouchable. A buzzy, discordant, unhappy wave swept rapidly from her lumbar spine up to her temples, and she rocked gently from side to side as she walked. They had come to the front steps of a computer lab.

"I've got to study," said Clara. "How about you?"

The question was for show; Clara and Clara alone knew that Alice had taken to staying up all night every third day or so, studying voraciously then and only then. Alice shook her head.

Clara did it again, then, one last time. Looked Alice over then pulled her in for a hug. Alice felt wet tears against her face. As she withdrew, Clara took Alice's hand.

"You need help, baby," she said, then headed up the stairs. After a few steps up, though, Clara half turned and said something. All

Alice heard was wind, or perhaps it was the roar of her own blood pumping through her body. Either way, Clara's words remained obscure.

"They will always come for you," Clara seemed to say, and Alice knew that it was true.

Six

The tiled floor of the drab suburban hospital was light gray with a sickly olive stripe running wide down the middle. Being dragged down the hallway by her panicked mother Alice thought of the stripe as a conveyor belt and she the conveyed. She counted the scuffs from gurneys and wheelchairs as she passed by. Her mother's grasp on her wrist got tighter and tighter until her press-on nails threatened to draw blood. Alice, intent on the tile, felt nothing.

The waiting room was mostly empty and permeated with that unease typical of emergency rooms, that feeling that the staff are always either overreacting or underreacting. A man sat with his right foot wrapped in a crude bandage, propped up on a black duffel bag; Alice was momentarily disturbed to notice that he was holding his severed big toe between his middle finger and thumb. This would seem to be worthy of concern from both him and the staff, and yet he sat undisturbed, and the nurses and orderlies who puttered around seemed almost proudly indifferent. They were, however, clearly annoyed by the entreaties of a hysterical woman who was crying for help. Alice was intrigued when she remembered that this woman was her mother.

The triage nurse was a severe white woman whose uniform was distinguished by the peculiar addition of a hairnet.

"Please, help," said Alice's mother. "My daughter needs help."

The triage nurse kept her eyes on her small square computer screen just long enough for her lack of concern to register. Then she asked, redundantly, "Can I help you?"

"My daughter is very sick." Alice's mother spoke in a ragged voice between a gasp and a whisper. "She's very sick."

"Sick how? Sick in what way?"

Alice tried to pull away from her mother, but the fingers on her wrist were iron. Her mother pulled her close until their torsos were touching.

"She's having problems." There was a struggle in that old, familiar face. Alice watched her mother lose some sort of minor war within herself. At last her mother hissed, "Psychological problems."

The triage nurse again waited a little too long to react, eyes moving from Alice to her mother and back.

"How old is she?" she asked.

Alice began to answer but her mother cut her off, squeezing her wrist hard enough that Alice saw stars.

"She's nineteen."

"Fill these out," the nurse said.

Alice's mother grabbed the clipboard. She muscled Alice over to the chairs. Alice considered this an unnecessary amount of force given how compliant her body was, on the whole. But then, she pondered the question of whose body it really was. They sat across from another mother and child, a little boy of perhaps six slumped over against his mom, who couldn't have been much older than Alice was herself. She found that she could not look at them, and so she leaned dramatically back, arching her spine so that she could count the individual ceiling tiles above them. Her mother was engrossed in the forms, but when she glanced over and saw how badly Alice was contorting herself in the chair her eyes went wide.

"Stop that!" she said, slapping Alice's hand instinctively. Alice only giggled, sitting upright but now bouncing her knees rhythmically to a tune only she could hear. As she grew more animated her mother scowled deeper and moved the pen faster and faster. Finally she scribbled her last scribble, then stomped back up to the triage desk.

"Done," she said, slapping the clipboard onto the desk.

"Is she insured?" said the triage nurse, making no move to collect the paperwork.

"She's on her father's insurance," said Alice mother, voice shaking. "I put the information in the form."

"Have a seat and we'll call you," said the triage nurse, turning to her computer, still not touching the clipboard.

"How long?" said Alice's mother. She was grasping the edge of the desk strongly enough that her hand shook.

"Have a seat, and we'll call you," said the triage nurse, giving Alice's mother a look of lazy disapproval.

Alice's mother returned to her seat. She was pleased to find that her daughter was simply sitting there, arms pulled into her hoodie with folded hands peeking out into her lap. Her gaze was far away, distant. Alice was wrapped up inside her own mind, her thoughts tying her consciousness in a knot, incredibly intricate and impossibly tight. She was trying to reason herself out of obsession and found that thoughts can never unthink a paranoid fixation. She had become convinced, by a comment on Instagram that must surely have been written in code, that an acquaintance from high school was conspiring to drain her campus dining card of funds. Alice was not yet certain of the ultimate plan, but the telltale signs were there. She had called Sadie in California at 6:00 a.m. Oklahoma time and asked for the girl's phone number. Sadie sounded sleepy and concerned and asked to know why, but Alice feared making her an accessory to what might eventually transpire.

Armed with the number she had texted the bewildered former classmate, keeping her texts arch and elliptical to avoid leaving a paper trail. But the confused responses infuriated Alice, and she was composing her grand accusation when her mother unlocked the door with a butter knife, wrenched the phone from her hands, and dragged her rail-thin body toward the car.

Now she was trying to figure out exactly how far the conspiracy went, how exactly she had let her accounts get compromised.

She had taken to checking her dining card's balance several times an hour, but it only showed the "right" amount, the erroneous balance remaining, and not the drained account she knew was due to appear anytime now. Besides, they had been chipping away at her funds for a long time, she had come to find. Finals week was only ten days away, and yet the five hundred or so dollars left seemed pitifully slim. Then her parents had come to take her home, away from school, when she was so close to the finish line of the greatest academic achievement of her life. When her mother walked in she stared at Alice's collarbone, which had become hard to miss, and cried fat tears while she said that she had been told that Alice was in trouble. Her father stood mute in the background and hadn't so much as hugged her since. It wasn't long before Alice's insomnia, excitability, and paranoia made it clear to her mother that it was time to seek help.

Alice's reverie in the ER was turning and turning, the cyclical thoughts of dark actors with dark purposes working against her developing their own momentum, a certain rabid logic. Perhaps it would have been safest to hide there, in the machinery of obsession, but then Alice's mother touched her shoulder and tried to speak.

Alice was snapped out of her fixations and now felt only fear, raw, animal fear, the urge to flee, her caveman brain crackling with electricity, and she bolted upright and started to sprint for the door. But her mother, acting on animal instincts of her own, moved with frightening speed and caught Alice by the hood of her sweatshirt. Against her daughter's protestations she wrestled them back toward the chairs.

"Do you see this?" shouted Alice's mother to the triage nurse, in a grimly triumphant tone. "Do you see that my daughter needs help?" But the triage nurse was talking to an orderly and did not turn. So Alice's mother forced Alice into a chair and kept her fingers latched around her wrist, where they would remain. And then they waited.

And waited. And waited.

A half hour, an hour, two. They sat and sat. Others came, signed in, and were seen. Eventually Alice saw the man with the missing toe limping out toward the parking lot, crutch under his arm. Every time they were jumped in line, Alice's mother swore and muttered. Again and again, she dragged Alice back to the desk to ask why her daughter wasn't being treated.

"You have to be patient," said the triage nurse, each time. It was a dance Alice would come to learn well: If you were sick enough to be dangerous, they'd ship you off to the local psychiatric hospital; if you weren't, they would try and wait you out. Every moment waiting was a moment to contemplate whether you were really sick, whether coming to the hospital was a mistake. If you calmed down enough while waiting, they felt no obligation to treat you. If you gave up and left, even better.

And indeed, over the course of three hours one of the most dangerous things for any psychotic patient happened to Alice: she calmed down. The immediate psychotic impulses ebbed. It was now very late at night and she became tired. Her thoughts slowed. Her fixations and paranoia throbbed on, but drained of their vitality by her deepening exhaustion they were overpowered by the ever-present human impulse to be okay. And just as soon as the wave of her overpowering emotions had crashed back down, so that now she was cognizant enough to at least look back at the crest and see it for the moment that it was, a nurse walked over to the two of them, squinted sideways at her clipboard, and told Alice's mother it was time.

The nurse led them into an examination room. She directed Alice to stand on the scale.

"How tall are you, darling?" she asked. Alice dutifully reported that she was 5'6. When the nurse moved the thing on the scale and announced "105," for the first time that evening Alice thought of her mother, and felt she could almost hear her shudder from the other side of the room. She spared a moment of regret for her mother; there was nothing in the world that Alice hated more than to make other people worry over her. This guilt could not however overwhelm her desire to keep going down and break a hundred pounds. She grasped the sides of the scale to keep from falling, then was led by the hand back to the table.

The nurse placed a little clip on Alice's finger to measure her pulse, then fitted her with a blood pressure cuff. She dutifully filled in values on the computer, then asked Alice about any allergies or medications.

"None," said Alice and her mother in unison. The nurse chattered away on the keyboard.

"Drugs or alcohol?" said the nurse. Alice felt the heat of her mother's glance on her neck.

"I drink sometimes," she said.

"Are you sexually active?" It got better and better.

"Sure," said Alice.

"How many partners in the past six months?"

"Two," she lied.

"The doctor will be with you shortly," the nurse said as she headed out the door.

"When?" asked Alice's mother, getting comfortable in her anger.

"Soon," said the nurse, and she was gone.

Alice sat on the little paper-covered table, her feet dangling down in front of her. Her mother ignored a nearby chair and paced around the room for the next twenty-five minutes. Finally in walked the ER shrink, the first of many ER shrinks who would walk into Alice's life with similar diffidence.

He looked like they all do, like they all would. His very serious glasses sat perched on a very serious nose that tied together a very serious face. His sandy-brown hair grayed at the temples; his fitted, well-ironed dress shirt fit snugly on a runner's frame. His face, to Alice, was not a face. The eyes that bore into her were ringed with condescension and pity. He looked like the kind of doctor who would patiently explain the theory of humours to a frenzied patient, like your favorite librarian, like the professor who you thought was cool until he savaged your final paper in his endnote comments. He looked bored, sharp, poised, distant, aloof, not unkind. He wore a brassy wristwatch with a dull leather band and a tasteful steel wedding ring. He studied his clipboard for a long while, hovering there, unhurried and unconcerned. Alice could feel her mother's tension rising as she waited and feared an explosive outburst was coming, but just as the tension crested he spoke.

"What seems to be the problem?"

Alice waited for her mother to say something, one beat two beats three. When she finally made up her mind to speak, her mother was busy interrupting her. "She thinks things she shouldn't think. She hears things and she paces around at night. She thinks her friends are plotting to kill her. I think she's been having unprotected sex."

The ER shrink only tilted his head perhaps half an inch toward his right shoulder. He studied Alice like a golfer studies the fairway while choosing a club.

"Well," he asked Alice, "what kind of thoughts have you been thinking?"

Alice rose to speak, then held her breath. It was a very good question. But where a few hours earlier she would have let it all spill out, the obsession and the paranoia and the thoughts that intruded into every element of her mind, now she was composed enough to explain in terms she felt would be better understood. Underneath, her mind raced in the same drunk circles, thoughts piling up against each other like a chain-reaction car accident in the snow. But she had coasted down ever so slightly from the peak of whatever hellish cycle she was in, and had rediscovered an emotion that can be immensely dangerous to those who would do best to share their unquiet minds: she felt embarrassed.

Still, she would not lie.

"Just everything has been moving fast, lately," she said. "I fixate on stuff, like my skin, my weight. I worry all the time. Like I worry about if I have enough gas to make it home even though

I just filled the tank. I worry that I didn't submit my homework online when I know I did. Sometimes I can't sleep. I feel pretty anxious."

Alice realized then that her mother had been holding her breath the whole time. The shrink still unmoving, Alice's mother began shaking her head in the silence, pawing her foot in front of her like she was trying to stamp out an imaginary fire. A dull high noise squeaked from her mouth, but it seemed to take forever for her to form actual words. Her head was still shaking, now rhythmically, and Alice felt she might explode if the words did not finally come, and just then they came.

"That's not it," her mother cried. "She's not being honest! It's not forthright!"

Alice could not help but chuckle at the word, and she searched the shrink's face for similar amusement, but he never twitched.

"My daughter is not well," said Alice's mother, and now she was finally, fully crying, big wet tears, and this time Alice was able to summon up some real pity for her.

"She's not well," she said again, wiping her tears with a scented pink Kleenex. "She ruined all of her friendships. She has no one to room with next year at school. She checks the driveway for surveillance vans. Her first semester grades were terrible. She counts the silverware before she goes to bed. Her friend Sadie got caught with *drugs*. She's not well."

Alice turned the words over in her head, trying to feel them out. She could not quite define the shape of them, their contours, the way she had been doing with words for a while. She had always been a secret syllable counter, she(1) had(2) al(3) ways(4) been(5) a(6) syl(7) la(8) ble(9) count(10) er(11), going back to childhood, but lately she had taken to running words through a far more extensive apparatus, like a factory in an old cartoon, squeezing them, prodding them, turning them over like rocks in a tumbler. But now, sitting in that room exhausted, with that man's presence hanging around them like a blank faced Buddha, she could not bring herself to really engage with her mother's words, in fact felt like it had been a very long time since she had ever analyzed words in that manner, couldn't quite recall how the process went. For months words had danced in her brain, whether she wanted them to or not, but that night, exhausted and peering out at her life as if through a window, "she's not well" sat dead and leaden in her hands.

The shrink shuffled around, eyes on Alice.

"I'd like to speak to Alice alone, Mom," he said.

Alice braced herself for an outburst, but none came. Her mother merely shuddered a bit, then rose to her feet, studying the ground. She lightly grasped Alice's skinny wrist, squeezing it gently, then shuffled out of the room.

Once she was gone, the doctor's demeanor changed. He grabbed a chair and turned it around so that he was sitting on it backwards, like a cool teen in a high school movie. He leaned back and clutched the clipboard against his chest.

"Let's try again," he said.

Alice briefly met his gaze and then found it very hard to keep doing so. She stared at the floor instead. She knew this was some kind of a chance, but didn't know what kind, and anyway she suddenly found herself afflicted with dry mouth. She shrugged.

He clicked his pen in and out.

"Okay, let's try it this way," he said, affecting a let's-get-real tone. "How often do you take Adderall?"

It was not a question Alice was prepared for. She stammered out a denial.

"Look, I'm not the cops or a dean at ou," he said. "You're very thin, wouldn't you say?"

She would not say thank you. She felt healthy for the first time, felt that her real body had emerged from a chrysalis. She also felt indignant, offended, but struggled to find words.

"I guess so," she said.

"Mmhmm," said the shrink. "Doing well in school?"

She felt swept along in a conversation she did not want to have and only wanted to end. She surrendered to his vision of her mental state.

"Yes, doing very well in school."

"Yeah," he said, looking pleased with himself. He scribbled on his form.

"Look, Alice," he said, rising again and leaning against a counter, again clutching the clipboard against his chest.

"I want to be real about this. We see it a lot—young woman, no real history of trouble, goes off to school, feels the pressure, comes home skinny and paranoid. You can see where my mind is going."

Alice nodded, fixated by a spot on the wall. She could not in fact see where his mind was going; she had only a loose grasp on where her own mind was going.

"So?" he said.

"So," said Alice.

"So," said the shrink, "how often do you take Adderall?"

Alice considered the question. She had, in fact, taken a few pills a couple times, early in her college career. And she had done coke with Sadie. But she had not done any kind of speed in months, had no need for it, looked down on anyone who did. She had been flying for months, burning only her own fuel, and could not imagine needing help gathering energy, even less taking such a foreign substance into her body when contaminants and saboteurs were everywhere.

But she looked at his expectant face and felt tired, so tired, and could not stand to fight it out with him.

"Once in a while," she said, declaring surrender.

He snapped a self-satisfied head nod.

"That's what I thought," he said. "So what, once or twice a week? Every night?"

And now Alice, still pummeled by relentless and circular thoughts, was compelled to find just the right way to respond. Going to rehab sounded like hell.

"Like once a week," she said. He scribbled.

"Tonight?"

"Sure," she lied.

"Okay," he said. "So you get used to it, you take it a little more often than you should, you go home, you pop a couple, you get paranoid and freak out your mom."

He was nodding to himself now, looking serene, eyes glittering behind his Warby Parkers. Alice felt she could do nothing but murmur, not quite words, but assenting nonetheless.

"And you'd prefer me to keep this from your mother," said the shrink.

Alice could think of nothing she wanted more than to bolt from the room, to stride purposefully through the halls of the hospital and out the door, into the night, leaving the doctor and his patient patronizing tone to sputter. Instead she simply nodded her head yes.

"Okay," he said. "We can keep this to ourselves. But we gotta talk about these drugs."

And so Alice gave one of the great nodding and murmuring performances of her life, looking by turns thoughtful, pensive, concerned, and resolved, all in line with his expectations. He told her that just because it's a prescription drug, doesn't mean it's not dangerous; that it's easy to build up a dependence; that some users of prescription stimulants even turn to cocaine. He emphasized the word, stabbing a finger at his clipboard as he did so, and Alice made sure to make her most somber face. Eventually, she was agreeing that she would throw out her pills and talk to an addiction specialist if she felt she could not stop. Satisfied, he made one last authoritative scribble on his clipboard.

"Was there anything else?" he asked.

Alice paused. She wanted so much to go home and sleep, but a muted alarm was sounding in some deep recess of her brain, an impulse to save herself that she almost missed among the ceaseless clarions of paranoia, which signaled that someone was trying to kill her.

"The thoughts, I can't keep up," she said, suddenly feeling flushed and hot. "They invade. I build a fortress but they invade. I think things on top of other things I'm thinking. They pulse and shimmer. I feel I can solve every equation that's ever been put on paper. The math, I'm not afraid of it anymore, I feel I've been given mastery and dominion over it. I am blooming, violently. The world is my chrysalis. I'm so, so scared to go to bed and wake up to find the enemy in my room."

He stood, a blank. Alice waited for him to note something on his clipboard.

"You're very tired," he said softly.

Alice felt the briefest urge to resist, then surrendered completely.

"Yes, very tired," she said.

"Let's get you home and in bed then," he said, then reached for the door. "Let me take care of Mom."

The shrink led Alice's mother back into the room. Alice felt a sudden wave of concern and pity for her mother, who looked exhausted, her mascara halfway dribbled down her face from crying. She stood with her hands under her armpits, staring intently at the psychiatrist.

"Your daughter's very tired," he said, sounding his most authoritative and patient. "She's been dealing with a lot of stress. She needs uninterrupted sleep. I recommend melatonin."

"No," said Alice's mother, crying again. "No, no, no. She's not well. She needs real help."

The psychiatrist typed into the exam room's computer for a moment.

"I'm prescribing her a sedative, enough for a week or so," said the doctor.

"She needs help," said Alice's mother, again.

"She could use some therapy, I agree," he said. "There are resources on the hospital's website."

With that, he gathered his papers and started to head out of the room.

"Good luck, Alice," said the shrink. "And get some rest."

When he had gone, Alice was left with her quietly murmuring mother, a prescription for hydroxyzine, and—though now constrained by the numbing power of exhaustion—she was left with all the thoughts her mother had referred to, the thoughts she knew she should not think.

Seven

In later years Alice would wonder why her mother had not in fact sought outpatient care for her, therapy if nothing else, following that first experience with emergency mental healthcare. Perhaps it was the perceived cost at a time when, she would later learn, her parents were struggling. Perhaps the thought of navigating the insurance hurdles was too much to bear. Perhaps small-town Oklahoma didn't offer enough options for care. Or perhaps the emergency room doctor's icy condescension and self-assured certainty had simply overwhelmed Alice's mother. One way or another, there were no later doctor's visits, no second opinions. Alice's mother called the hospital once and got a refill of the sedatives, which she then dutifully forced on Alice exactly in time with the recommended dosage, but otherwise the only treatment Alice received was confinement, exile. And, against all odds, eventually it seemed to work.

For two months Alice paced around her room, at first almost exclusively broken only by trips to the bathroom or kitchen. She would walk from one corner to the other, counting her steps, and see how many she could take before stealing to the window to watch for any shadowy individuals that were surveilling her. She scribbled diligently in a notebook, explaining to herself and the world the many ways in which human systems interrelated and overlapped, the nexus of action and intent, and all of it leading to her persecution, the society-wide communal effort to stop her from becoming what she was meant to become. She watched endless hours of daytime TV and developed a prediction system for who would win in the various judge shows (*People's Court*, *Judge*

Judy, Divorce Court) based entirely on body language and timber of voice. The system was almost always wrong. In time her mother invited her to the garden to help her pull weeds; in time she invited Alice to the store.

For long weeks that seemed to stretch out more than they had since she was a child, Alice sweated in her little room as the underpowered AC unit in the window struggled to cool even that small space. She read through half of her stack of *Baby-Sitters Club* books, some thirty of them, and found them comforting until one day she found them only tiring and stopped. The wound she had dug into her side, be it a sore or an abscess or something else, gradually healed, though a spongy lump would always remain, and she would at times gently run a finger over its mass. She found the willpower to stop digging into it in her fear of another trip to the ER with her mother. She masturbated constantly and sent texts to try and cheer up Sadie, who was in a parent-enforced exile of her own.

Gradually the endless beating waves of thoughts, the torrent, the deluge, slowly faded, though the force would ripple back up and down, throbbing, the whole summer. She still obsessed, still worried, still saw chaos and danger around every corner, but in time these fears came less constantly and gripped her less intensely. She had work to do. Despite thriving for most of her second semester, she had taken two incompletes, and both professors had made sure to let her know what a favor they were doing for her. Both required her to complete twenty-plus page papers "as soon as possible" to receive her credits. But where she had previously stayed up until dawn writing and rewriting her papers, exceeding the requested page counts to the point that her professors had to ask her gently to stop, as the summer petered on she found it harder and harder to summon the energy to do her school work. To her immense unhappiness she gained ten pounds, though she remained thin. She did squat thrusts and jumping jacks until she was dizzy but over time she fleshed out nonetheless, and the clothes that had hung off of her for months began to fit again.

She and her mother barely spoke at the beginning, but in time warmth returned to their relationship. The weekend after her ER visit her mother informed her that her father wanted to have "a talk." When they sat down for it at the kitchen island he stared red-faced into his coffee, let out a few words about the family being there for each other, asked her to be patient with her mother, and then switched to discussing the approach of tulip-planting season with enthusiasm. The whole thing took perhaps two minutes, and the rest of their summer conversations were restricted to OU football, reminding her to take out the trash, and his beloved tulips.

Alice had taken to pressing flowers and leaves in the pages of her thick college textbooks, which she hoped to sell back in the fall. The process took forever, and she complained to her parents that she would never make anything at the rate things were going. A few days later she came down from her bedroom for breakfast and found a small press sitting in a box from Amazon; you took your flowers and leaves and greenery and placed them between the pads of the press, clipped it shut, and then put it in the microwave for thirty seconds. She burned two sets of beautiful petals before bothering to read the instructions and only then learned that she had to reduce the microwave's power by half. In a few hours she felt that she was a professional at the pressing of flowers, though she still burned more flowers than she should have, and she had come to turn her mind from process to composition. The first creation that she considered official was made up of only a single flower and some pressed cilantro used to represent the vegetation the flower grew out of, glued to a piece of white poster board. She considered it a triumph of negative space. Eventually she learned that using adhesives was considered amateurish in the flower pressing community, and she arranged a special trip to the local big-box craft store for some clear acrylic panes and frames they could fit inside. She would press her materials and delicately compose them and then sandwich them between the panes. Her mother praised her effusively and insisted on hanging a half dozen of them around the house. Alice dreamed of making one for a sensitive and reserved boy with muscles who would gallantly pick her up and put her to bed when she got too drunk.

As the fall semester drew closer Alice found that her mind was often quiet. She was still gripped by strange impulses and taken to mood swings, but then, she was a teenager. Her mother was at last willing to talk about Alice returning to school. Alice strategically did not mention to her parents that Sadie was, to Sadie's great despair, transferring to OU. Her parents had told her that they would not pay for her to go to school in Los Angeles anymore, with its partying and drugs. Sadie's protests that OU was full of partying and drugs only served to prod her parents into contemplating keeping her out of school altogether. Alice felt oddly hollow when Sadie first told her that they would share a school, a campus, and presumably a social life, but as the summer dwindled her happiness grew. It had been a long and lonely first year. She would write and delete an email to Clara a dozen times. The trouble was that she felt there was so much to say, but she likewise felt unable to articulate any of it. She felt too that she owed Clara some kind of apology but could not recall for what. She did know she missed Clara, and she knew that they would never be close again, and her life felt as small as her room.

Despite all her introspection that summer, despite all her time spent only on thinking, Alice was unable to think about her thoughts. She knew in some dim sense that she had gone to the ER, but the reasons for that visit stayed tantalizingly out of frame, they were something she could not resolve, could hardly begin to investigate, let alone analyze. She knew in some strange sense that she was in recovery but could not bring her brain to define what she was recovering from. She could not visualize the face of the psychiatrist, so all that remained was her sense that he was profoundly unimpressed, and in time she simply did not think of the hospital at all. When school started again it would be Alice's second year, but she would not yet be a sophomore, and here too that fact hung around her consciousness without her ever being able to interrogate why.

Two weeks before Alice was set to return to campus, her mother began making noises about a leave of absence and staying home for the fall semester. Alice felt a sweep of panic at the idea and a simultaneous pang of attachment to her room, to reading, to arts and crafts, to the quiet existence she had enjoyed for the prior three months. But a summer was one thing, four more months something else, and Alice was tired of her mother's control and her father's unhappiness. It was money that won the fight; she had put down a deposit on her dorm room, some fees had been paid, and Alice asserted without knowledge but with considerable enthusiasm that to take a semester off would imperil her financial aid. Her mother got over it in a couple of days. After all, Alice was back to acting like a typical late adolescent, lonely and bored, skinny and disheveled, but no longer describing vast and florid conspiracies to drain her bank account, to arrest her triumphant rise, to sap her power.

Though she was increasingly happy that Sadie would be joining her in ou, they were not rooming together. Alice had come to believe that she had to live in a single. It was more expensive, and her parents could not pay, so she was taking out more loans, which dimly concerned her, but her experiences with Clara had convinced her that she was best off alone, in her own space. Especially on those nights she wanted to stay up late. This had come to be her understanding of why she and Clara had gone so wrong: Alice was an only child. Surely that was why they could not make it work. Sooner or later, Alice was sure, she would write that email to Clara. She would even send it.

Writing was on her mind a good deal the last week of summer. She was consumed by the desire to put words down. She felt like this pocket of time at home, carved out of the flow of the life she had imagined for herself, was a time to *create*, never mind that the term papers she needed to submit to get credit and become a sophomore were still unwritten. She sat down and started composing in the notepad application on her laptop, enjoying the rhythms of her fingers on the keyboard. She was resolved to write and write and when her story was told seek out an agent and publish to great fanfare, and then on to the Hollywood treatment. The words came naturally.

The story she wrote was about a young woman who was babysitting for a toddler on a late October evening in a grand old farmhouse. The young urban professional parents were off to dinner and a show. The protagonist had fed the toddler and read her a story and put her to bed, then retired to the couch to read on her own. But little did she know that a goblin had crept up to the window of the toddler's bedroom and opened it, beckoning her with a crooked finger. And the toddler had clambered up and out of the window and walked in the dying light of day toward the deep dark woods a football field's length away. And the babysitter had glanced out the window in passing and to her shock and horror saw the little toddling shape, moving unsteadily but with purpose toward the forest, white shirt vivid against the patchy and darkening green of late-dusk grass. The babysitter rushed to catch the child but could not reach her before she came to a small crack in the earth and, giggling, climbed inside. The babysitter held her breath and squeezed painfully into the underearth to follow her charge; she found an enchanted world inside, a vast catacomb populated by elves and fairies and all manner of fantasy creatures, and always she could not quite catch the toddler, who remained just out of reach and then just out of sight. And in the end she came to a grand hall, bedecked in gold and jewels, and an entire royal court, ostrich lords, halfling duchesses, a pixie for a jester. On a stately throne sat a half-man, half-bison, who looked wise and who regarded the babysitter coolly.

What will you give me, to recover this child? asked the king.

She is not yours to ransom, said the babysitter. The king sat unmoved. The babysitter reached into her pocket and found the bottle opener on her keychain. She slid it from its ring.

This is cold metal, worthy of a king, she said. She held it high so that it could glint in the torchlight.

The deal is fair, said the king, and the babysitter walked gingerly to where he sat and placed it in his furry palm. He blessed the child with a kiss and then handed her delicately to the babysitter. He motioned, and a door opened in the wall, and behind it was a staircase lit only by fire. And up the stairs she carried the toddler, who cooed and giggled, and they emerged at the end of the field, and though it had been hours it was somehow still twilight, and they returned home, and the babysitter placed her in her crib and watched her drift off to sleep. And in time the parents came home and paid her fifty dollars and she said nothing of her adventure, but would for the rest of her life look for cracks in the earth where she might find the courts of kings.

When the story was complete, Alice was sure she had completed her life's work. She briefly considered not returning to college. She began researching how to sell a novel. When she saw the page range for a typical novel, she realized that she had no idea how long it was, given that it was prepared in the notepad, and briefly wondered if she would have to split the story in two. When she copy and pasted the story into a word processor she found that she had written twenty-seven pages.

She dug her suitcase out from under her bed and began to pack.

Eight

Her second year of college (not her sophomore year, not yet, she admonished herself) began with a crisp simplicity, a steady and reliable march of days organized around her classes. Her worries of being lonely in a single were not entirely unwarranted, but she found she took to it pretty well, thanking the stars that she had no romantic relationship to manage. She had few relationships to manage of any kind, really; she was friendly with some of her classmates and maintained cordial terms with a few people she had met the previous semester, but she was in no group texts, was not urged by anyone to pledge their sorority, and now felt close to only her mother and Sadie. And neither of those relationships was uncomplicated.

Sadie had of course settled into OU quickly and comfortably, pulling people in with her beauty and charm. Most of the few times Alice actually hung out in groups that fall semester, she was pulled along by Sadie; she could not help but note the irony of a transfer student helping a returning student make friends. But she was glad for Sadie and they fell back in with each other naturally. It even pleased Sadie's parents, who had been stung by her drug "arrest." (She had in fact been caught by an RA at USC and given a lecture by their public safety department, but never reported to the police.) Alice, good old reliable Alice, would help keep Sadie on the right path.

Alice did at times think of Clara. She went on wanting to mend fences. Some part of her knew, however, that it was better for both of them to remain apart, at least for now. She remained vaguely aware that she owed Clara many apologies but was still stymied when she tried to remember for what. This was not an entirely uncommon experience for her, in those months. She could barely remember going to the hospital, and what she could recall was mere images, the psychiatrist's face, her mother's mounting anxiety, the stained tiles in the ceiling. A couple times she ran into Clara and said hello, asked her how school was going. They were blessedly comfortable interactions, but each was a brief exchange of pleasantries before separating. Once Clara said, "You look good, Alice," before wandering away.

Alice could not entirely agree. The ten pounds she had gained in late summer turned into twenty by mid-semester. She admonished herself that this was simply a return to her ordinary weight, the weight she carried when she showed up on campus. She reasoned that this was a blessing, given how many of her peers had gained weight since moving in freshman year. But whatever part of her brain insisted that she was fat was not amenable to reasoning. She yearned to be the weight she had achieved in the spring, the weight that compelled her mother to dig her nails into Alice's side and worry. She yearned to feel the way she had felt when she was taking pictures of herself for Instagram nearly every day, yearned to have her high-school classmates comment "skinny queen" and for boys she never thought about to show up in her DMs. Now she took Instagram pictures of campus buildings and flowers.

The weight issue was an issue of desirability, and she also yearned for sex and affection if not for love, but the two were unrelated; she had no doubt that she could secure sex whenever she needed it and a boyfriend if she really desired, whatever her weight. To be a young woman in college meant an inbox full of clumsy come-ons, even from some rather attractive boys. But there was something in the way, some sort of block in her mind. The intense throbbing desire for sex, particularly for hot and dirty and shameful sex, had ebbed a great deal since the spring. All thoughts came slower now, and the urge to get fucked was less common and less insistent. But she did want sex, did want someone to hold her with strong arms and rough hands, not that many of the boys at ou had either. Besides, picking a boy and going through the work of securing a casual but caring ongoing sexual relationship seemed endlessly daunting to her.

She would write "daunted" in her notebook during Intro to Genetics and Evolution, which seemed goofy in retrospect but was not an inaccurate way to describe her life. Many things now seemed daunting where nothing had a few months prior. G&E was not as hard as her math course but was still giving her trouble. She was surviving with Bs in those two classes and As in her other three, but school felt like work again. She had settled into more or less ordinary sleeping habits, although she still was prone to staying up too late on her phone. The 3:00 a.m. writing sessions were a thing of the past. Alice knew it was healthier to sleep but could not help but sometimes miss the rush. The two final papers she needed to turn in to convert Incompletes into grades remained unfinished; dozens of times she had opened the files and found that the task in front of her seemed impenetrable.

But all in all it was a quiet, content semester, an unremarkable and pleasant progression of classes, lunches with Sadie, and phone calls home. Her mother had let her know that Alice was back in her good graces via her particular kind of parent-to-child telepathy. Alice went to the gym regularly for the first time in her life, though the weight never came off. She wrote a little, odd notes and random splashes of fiction, and thought about posting some of it online. She even avoided getting her annual fall cold.

She sank into college and all of its lovely cliches. She kept her world on campus artificially small; on the right day she could pretend that she went to school in a tiny New England town, a little liberal arts college instead of a vast intimidating educating machine, and somehow she kept casually thinking that in a few months snow would arrive.

When Halloween arrived, she felt her social isolation a little more than usual. For the first time in her life she had no costume picked out. She was somewhat offended that she had no plans, though she could not say who that offense was directed at, and anyway would likely have declined any invitations.

The Saturday before Halloween, late at night, she got a message on Instagram. It was from Evan. The first communication from him since the night she lent him a hand in his car, though they had occasionally liked each other's photos.

"Long time," he said.

Alice, for a moment, wished desperately that she was still sharing a room with Clara.

"A year," she said.

He sent her an emoji doing some sort of smile and wink, the intent of which was lost on Alice. She threw her phone on the bed and headed down the hall to take a shower.

When she returned, she found he had messaged again.

"I think about you a lot," he said.

"So often that you didn't talk to me for a year," she said, then busied herself cleaning her dorm for a half hour before checking again. Again, an inscrutable emoji.

"I don't know what that means," she replied. "It's late, Evan."

"I want to see you," came the immediate reply. She browsed the web on her phone for a bit.

"Cool," she said. "I read in the café in Bizzell every Tuesday and Thursday after Anthro."

"I mean tonight," he said. "Now."

And so he forced the issue. She breathed out quickly in irritation. She looked out the window, as if searching for the answer to the question that presented itself: Really? Him? That guy? He wasn't even that cute. She grudgingly went to war with herself, debating what she really wanted, but in the end it was a symbolic defense. Yes, him. That guy. Really.

"I thought you had a girlfriend."

"No, that's over," he said. "Way over."

She frowned and wondered briefly if this was true. She pulled up his Instagram feed and found that, for several weeks now, it was free of any pictures of his girlfriend, a cheerful-looking South Asian girl who was, if she was being honest, too cute for him. She dug a bit and found her account. There too the pictures together had stopped weeks back, and as she had many more photos than he did it made her feel more confident. But there was no smoking gun either way. It would have to do, though. She was not entirely confident he was telling the truth, but she was sure she had done enough due diligence to satisfy her obligation to the other girl. She thought about how long it had been since she had been pinned to a mattress under a heavy dude body.

She texted him her dorm and room number.

"If you're not here in a half hour I'm going to sleep."

Thankful that she had just showered and done a bit of cleaning, she pondered how much primping she could do in thirty minutes, and then just how much she felt he deserved. Not much, was the easy decision. She applied a little makeup dutifully and changed from loose pink sweatpants to casual but tight leggings. The last thing she wanted was for him to think she had gotten dressed for him. She got more and more nervous at the minutes passed, then firmly annoyed when he broke her half-hour rule by twelve minutes. Then a light rap on her door.

He was standing squinting under the hallway overheads. Her own room was lit by fairy lights and a couple of candles, which were firmly prohibited in her dorm.

"Hey," she said.

"Hey gorgeous," he said, then leaned in to kiss her, grabbing for her breast at the same time.

"No," she said firmly, pulling the errant hand down and tugging him into her room.

"It's not going down like that, and you don't think I'm gorgeous."

He made awkward throat noises and shifted his weight from one foot to the other.

"Not tonight, you don't," she said, with evident sadness in her voice. "Maybe someday I'll care enough to show you gorgeous."

She pulled him to her bed and instructed him to sit. She sat cross-legged with a good foot of distance between them.

"There should be no lies between us," she said, then regretted it. It was an honest statement of intent but then he was a dumb drunk adolescent boy who could not possibly understand what she wanted and may not have cared if he did. And she hated sounding grandiose.

"Oh, yeah, totally," he said.

She tried again: "Tell me what's been happening with you."

And he did, in fits and starts, occassionally clumsily attempting to make out with her but mostly getting the hint. They talked for a long time. When talk turned to her, she mostly deflected it back to him; this was a habitual reality of being a girl talking to boys, but also convenient for her. She could not think of how to talk about last semester or the summer, could not, in fact, even really recall what had happened beyond feelings and impressions. She listened patiently while he talked about his bitch calculus professor and his new band, and when she felt that they had gotten over a certain hump of mutual attention, she pulled off his pants.

She gave him head for a while, not her A-game but a solid enough effort. He returned the favor with mediocre but high-effort oral sex, until she caught herself nodding off, so she gently pulled on his hair.

"Come up here," she said, and he clambered on top of her, she felt the lovely weight of sex, and he fucked her. It did not last long, but she had fun, and when it was over he did that sweaty smiling out-of-breath boy-on-top-of-you thing, and she realized how badly she had needed it. They lay in bed panting for a bit, then spent ten minutes lying next to each other checking their phones. Eventually he yawned with his typical aggravating theatricality.

"Damn, I'm pretty tired," he said.

"I bet you are," she said. "I'll see you later."

"Damn," he said. "I didn't even ask to stay."

Alice decided to go with a little more tenderness.

"Do you want this to happen again?"

He blinked. While she waited, Alice cast a glance out the window and watched a slutty witch stumble toward the dorm; she felt a pang of concern for her, but at least she was coming home.

"Is that a trick question?" he stammered.

"No," she said, and put her hand on his hip. "I'm asking you if this was a one-time thing."

"No, no, I want to see you again."

It was exhausting. She was exhausted.

"But you don't want to, like, take me on a date."

He considered his shoes. Apparently they provided the answer he was looking for.

"No, I mean, that could be cool, yeah."

"Yeah," she said. "Look, Evan, I want to be able to do this when I want to, but I'm not going to be your 2:00 a.m. girl, and if you think I'm going to be that, you can fuck off."

"I get it, I get it," he said, and seemed more sober. "I'd love to get together next week, go for a walk, drink some beers."

How little it took, Alice thought. She kissed him on the cheek.

"Go home," she said. "Goodnight."

When he was gone she got herself off. As she did so she thought of the sexual encounter she had just had, the sex that had failed to produce the orgasm she was now prodding into existence. But orgasms had not been hard to come by now that she was living alone, while the wonderful visceral slightly threatening feeling of a boy's weight pressing down on her was.

She was almost overwhelmed by the desire to sleep, but found herself reaching into the big plastic tub where her flower pressing supplies were found. She fished out the microwave press her mother had given her. Drooping in her vase were hydrangeas and pansies, a present she had bought for herself a week before. She fetched several of each, carefully cut the heads from the stems, and laid them out delicately on the press before placing it in her microwave. She knew she was far too exhausted to arrange them that night, much less to secure them in a frame, but she also knew she had to save them right then, knew she had to take something delicate and preserve it forever while she could.

Nine

Alice's dorm room felt icy cold, and though it was the third week of February, Oklahoma was still Oklahoma and a dim far-off part of her mind estimated the actual temperature at no lower than fifty degrees.

"The 'scientific' temperature," she said with contempt, to no one, for no purpose, from her spot on the carpet. Of course both windows were open, and she conceded that this was not ideal from a temperature standpoint. But the point was academic; she had not moved, could not move. For hours she laid in the fetal position in the dead center of her room, had in fact moved her desk chair into the hallway to create room for this purpose. She had been confined largely to bed for days, but had moved with a certain sense of ceremony onto the harsh orange carpeted floor. It was what she felt she deserved and where she felt she belonged.

The simple pleasures and quiet living of the fall semester now seemed far away. As the season turned she found herself withdrawing even more, not even seeing Sadie for weeks at a time. She had been reading steadily for the past several months and enjoying it more than she had in a long time. But near the end of the semester she was beset by feelings of being overwhelmed by her workload and her little stack of novels had gone untouched. When she went home for Thanksgiving she rolled her eyes when her mother cried and talked about "getting her Alice back"—"get me back from what?" she had texted Sadie—but she played along and humored her mother as she gushed to Alice's favorite aunt and least-favorite uncle about her progress in school. But she had far less patience and far less energy when she went home for a month for break. She and her mother seemed to keep running into each other, physically and frustratingly, and both of them grew short with each other. Her father even intervened once, admonishing both for picking at each other, what must have been a Herculean effort for a man who seemed now to care about nothing else but OU's performance in the recent bowl season.

"I want you at service tomorrow morning," said Alice's mother. "I brag on you there and nobody believes it because you don't come."

"I can't tomorrow," said Alice. She was robotically washing dishes.

"Why?"

"Because I'm sleeping in." She squeezed another giant dose of detergent into the sink.

"Oh, stop," said her mother, grabbing at Alice's hands and tearing off the yellow rubber gloves. "You're not even pretending to do it right." She began furiously washing.

"You sleep in every day," she said. "You can give me a single Sunday."

"I don't believe in it."

Alice's mother slammed the pot lid she was cleaning down in the stainless steel sink, then again, then again.

"Well maybe your father and I don't believe in spending every last goddamn dollar on you! Lazy, goddamn ungrateful."

"That sentence needs a noun."

At that Alice's mother moved to smack her with the brush she was using to wash the dishes.

Alice fled to her room. She spent the following morning sleeping in. She was so tired, nowadays, and "nowadays" seemed to stretch further and further back . . . But the following week she volunteered to go to service, in a bid to mend fences, and though she almost fell asleep on the megachurch pew and did do so on the long car ride home, after the proceedings were over she summoned all of her charismatic energy and performed the role of chipper overachiever for her mother's friends and enemies.

She playacted an overworked but cheerful college student, self-deprecating but enviable, complaining about classes but sharing her success, portraying a ball of watch-out-world-here-I-come energy. She even turned it up when talking to the women she knew her mother did not like. Her mother had been so pleased she came home the following day with a bouquet of fresh flowers for Alice to press.

But the joy didn't last, and in that month she felt whatever optimism remained from the fall drain out of her system like blood from a sacrificial goat's neck. Her goal of getting started on next semester's reading came to seem totally preposterous. She spent long days lying on the couch watching cable, *Law & Order* and local news and her beloved judge shows, until eventually her mother's habitual theatrical sighs drove her up to her room for good. A request to take her dinner up there led to a screaming fight with her mother; her father's face had never looked so pained and vacant as it had that night. Alice grew so impatient with her mother that she contemplated driving off into the night, but of course there was nowhere to go. When it was time for her to go back to school it came as a relief to all involved. For the first time, Alice's mother did not make the drive, begging off because of a fundraiser for the local high school. Her father drove her to Norman in silence and gave her one of his brief awkward fierce hugs before driving away.

And so she found herself slowly suffocating in her tiny single dorm room. The semester was little more than a month deep but she had already missed a dozen classes. She slept more than she ever had but felt tired all the time. Evan had, at last, given up after months of inconsistency on Alice's part. She knew he wanted to be more than a hookup, and sometimes she gave him every reason to think he was, and then she would ignore his texts for days. She felt bad for him; she felt bad about everything. She knew she had to cut him loose but could not imagine summoning the energy to do so. Lately his texts had come less frequently and she wondered whether he might do her the favor of just going away on his own. She hated herself for it but could imagine no other way, in her condition. What exactly her condition was, she would have been hard-pressed to define.

The truth is that she had grown to hate herself for everything she was and did. She had gained another ten pounds, now officially thicker than when she started at OU, and she hated the way she looked. She had been awful to her mother and hated herself for that. She hated herself for struggling with calculus and for being awkward with a sweet boy who had tried to flirt with her after class. She hated herself for driving away Clara and hated herself for never sending that email. She hated her professors and she hated the bubbly idiot blondes who hung around waiting for football players and she hated the girls she longed to be friends with because she was terrified of speaking to them, and they reminded her of the friendships she wanted and could not have.

Most of all, she hated herself for hating herself. She hated how self-involved it seemed, pretentious and clichéd. She hated that she had succumbed to a type of narcissism people like her were not entitled to access. She knew she was not important enough to hate herself and she hated herself for not being able to stop hating herself.

And so now the bed had become the floor. It seemed both safer and more appropriate for her station, down there. She had her phone and occasionally moved to check it, managed to scrape together the energy to decline Sadie's invitation to lunch via text or halfheartedly search on YouTube, but eventually even her weak grasp on her phone seemed too high of a mountain to climb, and it lay uselessly on the floor next to its useless owner, occasionally buzzing impotently at her.

She could see the little digital alarm clock on her desk from her vantage point. The minutes seemed never to move and also to barrel forward with ruthless momentum. This was a problem, as she had two classes that afternoon, and she had sworn a dark unholy oath that she would attend. As the first class approached, she scheduled when she would climb up off the carpet, giving herself enough time to get a little dolled up for the baseball player who she had enjoyed a low-level flirtation with. The minute arrived and she did not stand. Only a shower, then, she thought, and set a new time. When that moment came and went she decided, okay, no shower, just time enough to get to class. And then the class's start time arrived and she thought that she would just be fifteen minutes late if she hustled. And then she gave up on her first class and went through the same progression with her second, and when the last minute of the second class had passed she remained in her spot. Worthless, she thought to herself. Worthless, worthless human. And she really had to pee.

She thought of a novel she had once read about an adventurous halfling and the busty sorceress who was his adventuring companion. They had come to a hidden valley ringed with majestic white-capped mountains, the river that had carved the valley glistening in emerald and blue, whitewater roaring as it pushed down past forests and glades. The valley was verdant and peaceful, filled with animals that lived in perfect balance with each other, and friendly unicorns grazed by woods edge while pixies lit the trails at dusk, their wings lapidary and glistening. The halfling and sorceress had come to the grand city at the foot of the mountain that boundaried the valley, and its alabaster walls rose taller than the tallest tree.

But inside they found that each and every resident had been trapped in a crystal shell, their faces blank, free of pain but also of joy, and they stood unmoving and lifeless in their many positions in the city, the baker crystalized while baking bread, the town guard in their armor, the children at school. And of course in the novel the halfling and the sorceress tracked down the evil wizard and broke his curse. Alice thought and thought and thought about the story that day and was confronted with a conundrum. She felt great jealousy for the crystalized people, felt that their condition was only to be envied: alive but not, with nothing expected of them, no feelings and no desires. Then she wondered whether she really wanted to share their condition or whether she already did.

That evening, when she ordinarily would have trudged to the dining hall, stuck on the floor, her willpower broke and she wet herself. Laying curled up she felt it soak her panties and leggings and trickle onto the carpet. An impulse to get ahold of herself washed over her, but she felt physically compelled not to move. It occurred to her that she would like to cry, but she could not summon the emotional resources to do so and did not feel that she deserved to. Instead she slept.

When she woke it was past 2:00 a.m. She rose groggily to a seating position. Her damp leggings reminded her of the mess she had made. She pulled off her clothes, wrapped a towel around her waist and pulled on a T-shirt, then trudged to the communal shower. She counted steps then, and where counting syllables was energetic, even joyful, counting steps was grim and deadening. One step two step three step four. Each felt slower than the last.

She was saddened to find that she was not alone, but the other girl paid her no attention. Alice undressed and showered; she could hear the other girl's iPhone playing hip hop. She found herself wishing that she had simply worn the clothes she had soiled into the shower to wash them too, but then it occurred to her that the other girl would have seen and known. She began to lean against the wall and slide down to the floor but forced herself to stop. She didn't know if she would have the ability to rise again.

Afterward she stuffed her urine-stained clothes deep into her hamper so no one could see, not that anyone would bother looking at her laundry at 2:00 a.m. She had less than half a load of laundry in there but no choice but to clean what she had. The laundry room was mercifully empty. She started the wash and thought of her favorite uncle. All along she assaulted herself with wave after wave of punishing thoughts, deriding herself for her pathetic weakness, her failure. When the dryer was running she sat on top of it and felt the pleasure of its warmth, its vibration. It lent her enough energy to pick up her phone.

I need help, she texted.

I know, baby, texted Sadie. *I know.*

The next morning Alice woke to the sound of Sadie pounding on her door.

"Come on, Alice," came her muffled voice. "It's Sadie, baby."

Alice opened her eyes but could not move. The room felt frozen once again. Dried spit caked the side of her mouth. She had fallen asleep with her phone in her hand again; she summoned the courage to waken it and saw a host of text messages, no doubt from Sadie. Sadie pounded again.

"Alice, get up," she said, starting to sound irritated. "We've gotta get you down there."

Alice braced herself, then rolled over onto her other side, facing the door. The floor seemed awfully far down.

"Hey," she called softly, to no effect, then louder. "Hey."

"Come on, sweets," said Sadie. "Let me in."

Alice considered the command and found it momentarily impossible. But she heard the plaintive notes in Sadie's voice and knew that she had done that, that she had provoked that sad, desperate tone in the voice of her strong, bold, wild Sadie. She winced to herself. Sadie had put on a good show since coming to Norman and was just as popular as she always had been, but Alice knew that something was wrong, and knew that she was the only one who knew. Sadie had been badly stung by her cocaine "bust," by leaving USC in shame, and by coming here, to the exact place she had always said she would never go. (A status they shared.) LA Sadie had worried Alice. Norman Sadie broke her heart. And now Alice heard the panic in Sadie's voice, felt how hard she was trying to force it down, and she felt depths of shame even greater than that which she had felt every day.

For Sadie, and for Sadie alone, she summoned the will to rise.

She stumbled over to the door and let Sadie in. Immediately Sadie hugged her tight, then studied her face for a moment.

"You look like shit, babe."

Alice mustered a half-smile. "I don't think psych patients are supposed to look glamorous."

"You're not a psych patient."

"Not yet."

"Stop it," said Sadie. "Grab your shower stuff."

Alice dutifully shuffled into the shower and undressed. Sadie stood leaning into the stall with her, halfway through the curtain. She commanded Alice to scrub, then to wash her hair. She stepped out for a moment to give Alice privacy; Alice felt the deep urge to sink to the floor of the shower again, and almost did. But she could not bear the thought of Sadie returning to find her in such a state. She turned off the water but remained in the stall for a moment to feel the pleasant steam.

Back in the room Sadie dressed her in leggings and a hoodie. She brushed the hair out of Alice's eyes, which carried thick dark bags beneath them from oversleeping.

"It's the clinic, not the counseling center," said Sadie. "Like we said."

"Okay," said Alice.

The clinic was quiet and nearly empty and was somewhat soothing in its drabness. Sadie and Alice sat on sickly green chairs that squeaked when they shifted their weight. A receptionist sat scrolling through her phone at the front desk. Across from them sat a freshman with a comically large bag of ice duct taped to his ankle. The whole place radiated a gentle stillness that perfectly fit Alice's mood, so she was annoyed to be called within ten minutes of sitting down.

As she rose, Sadie grasped her hand and pulled her in for a hug.

"You'll be fine," she said. "I'm here."

"I know," said Alice.

Alice was weighed and measured, had her blood pressure and pulse taken. She was saddened to see that she had gained more weight. The nurse handed her a gown as she headed out the door, which seemed like a strange anachronism; Alice could not remember when she had last worn a gown at a doctor's office. Within a few minutes a knock came at the door, and the doctor walked in.

He was older, maybe mid-sixties, with a kind laugh-lined face, glasses perched on a big red nose, a ring of white hair running from ear to ear. He looked to Alice like she imagined her mythical lost grandfather might look, her mother's father, a man who she knew was alive but who was not to be spoken of. He grinned when he saw her, a conspiratorial kind of smile, then pulled up a stool and sat across from her. He thumbed through a manilla folder for a moment before speaking. Alice would have felt perfectly at ease, had she not been so self-conscious about how her breasts bulged beneath the gown. Seeing how she reflexively pulled at the robe to better hide herself, he spoke.

"Yes, I'm afraid no one likes those," he said, in precisely the type of kindly tone his face had suggested. "But we find it's better than the alternative of patients having to pull their pants down on command."

Alice nodded, struggling to make eye contact.

"It's okay."

"Now, Alice," he said, rechecking his folder, "what seems to be the problem today?"

She smoothed out the gown again. She felt but could not say. She had a list of complaints, but they seemed suddenly distant, unclear and unworthy of a trip to the doctor. She could not say what she thought she deserved to feel and thus could not say what she didn't. But she had to try.

"I'm feeling hollow and like my life is pointless," she said, which was not quite right but the best she had. "I lie around my dorm all day because doing anything feels like more than I can handle. I'm failing all my classes. I feel bad and then I feel bad for feeling bad, for being so weak that I let myself feel bad. I just hate myself so much, all the time."

She gasped for a moment, shifting uncomfortably on the bed.

"I peed myself yesterday," she said, trying to let go and cry but finding it impossible. "I just couldn't imagine getting to the bathroom and I couldn't think of a reason not to."

The doctor ran his hand over his bald head, flipped around in his folder for a moment.

"Well," he said, with evident sympathy, "no one deserves to feel that way, and I'm sorry."

He reached into his pocket and retrieved a small pad.

"And the good news is, no one has to."

He scribbled on the prescription pad.

"Let's get some questions out of the way," he said. "Do you drink?"

Alice wished Sadie could sit with her, and felt that she would probably be allowed, but the thought of asking exhausted her.

"Sometimes, but barely at all this semester," she said. "Maybe five or six drinks all semester."

"That's good," he said. "How about drugs?"

"No," said Alice, weakly.

"Nothing?" he said. "Not even marijuana? Maybe sometimes?"

"I mean, yeah sometimes, but again not at all this semester."

"And these feelings that you've been having—did they start after you stopped? Did you stop suddenly?"

"No, I—I didn't—" She regrouped. "I really didn't smoke much even before. It wasn't a habit."

"Okay," he said. "Are you on any meds?"

"No," she said.

"Birth control?"

"No," she said after a moment. She had taken the morning after pill three times in six months, but it did not seem relevant. The doctor fortunately was absorbed in his pad.

"No cocaine, you're sure, now? None?"

"No."

"I wouldn't share anything you said to me with anyone, Alice," he said, adjusting his glasses. "I just need to know in order to help you."

"I don't do cocaine," she said, irritation creeping into her voice.

"Okay, okay," he said. "How are you sleeping? Having a hard time getting to bed?"

"I've never slept more," she said. "I sleep all day. It's all I do."

"And you're still very tired, aren't you," he said. "Aren't you?"

Alice leaned back and stared out the window. Outside the sun fell uselessly on water-starved grass. A lonely cloud worked slowly across the sky. She held on to resistance for a moment longer, then felt it break apart inside of her as her stores of mental energy were depleted.

"Yes," she said. "Very tired."

He nodded. Scratch scratch scratch went his pen. "Okay, big question," he said. "Do you ever get really happy and really hyper, really energetic and excitable? Not based on anything, just because?"

Alice's eyes drifted to the window again, but she caught herself. She considered the question as though through a telescope. She could sound out the words in her head and she knew their meaning but could not connect them with anything else in her brain. Some part of her mind, dim and distant, called out for attention, asked for attending to. But she looked at the doctor with his kindly face and heard the HVAC system hum in the background and she wanted only to take something and to hum along too. She had always hated the idea of psychiatric drugs, refused to consider them, but found now that she wanted nothing more than to take a pill and leave the floor of her dorm behind her. He started to speak, so she answered the actual, basic question he had asked her.

"No," she said. "I never get really happy."

"Good," he said, smiling. "Young lady, it's the twenty-first century. No one should have to feel the way you do."

He reached into his folder and peeled off the page of his prescription pad.

"This is something that's gonna take a little time, but when it gets going, you'll be feeling good as new."

He handed her the prescription, smiling beatifically again. She couldn't tell if he thought that he was handing her a precious gift, or if she thought that herself.

"It's called Effexor."

Ten

She was a wounded, hunted animal and though the night was hot the pavement felt cold on her bare feet. She moved in the dark spaces between buildings on campus, avoiding lights, alternating between running and staggering in rhythm with her waves of panic and fear. Around her all she saw were threats, demons, men lurking in the dark to rape and kill her. She threw her body against a wall, pressing into it in the hopes that she might camouflage herself like an octopus she had once seen in a documentary that changed its color with beautiful mastery. The cool grainy brick felt heavy and secure against her back and helped her regain her balance. But threats loomed everywhere. Ahead of her a group of students were ambling drunkenly down a quad. Alice bled from her hand where she had crushed a wine glass, splintering the stem and pressing shards into her palm, barely feeling it among the furious trumpets that sounded in her mind.

In her brain, though, her synapses fired with an alien and mechanistic kind of purpose; there was no chaos, only an immensely misguided order. Some deep bestial neurological structures fired inappropriately and stoked within her an instinct of brute survival. The fragile skeleton of her ego threatened to snap under the pressure of the animal forces that pressed down on her consciousness, her narrative mind sagging and distended beneath pitiless and grandiose feeling. She must run. She must run. She must run.

She moved directionless and yet with purpose, picking her way across the vast campus in fits and starts, stopping to pee beneath a tree and later to regroup under the awning of a locked building. Her phone buzzed constantly, as people in her life, even

Clara, responded to the dozens of text messages she had sent that night. Sadie called her again and again, and each time Alice looked at her phone she studied Sadie's picture as it rang, feeling as she did some deep need that she could not feed. The texts mounted, but where she was obsessively sending them an hour before she now could not bear to look. Everything she did, everything she thought, was freighted with importance, meant the difference between whether she would live or die, between whether the world would tumble on in scruffy glory or break apart into billions of indifferent shards.

Eventually she came upon an unlocked door. The building was lit up inside, as they all were, and some strange instinct compelled Alice to lament the carbon emissions. She crept along the hallway, gazing into the windowed doors, looking for threats, perhaps, or for something else, something less clear. She looked for classrooms to hide in but found only offices, tight little spaces occupied by cubicles and corporate wall art. She tested a door but found it locked, then another, and another, growing gradually panicked as she did so. When she found one slightly ajar she tumbled inside, falling to the ground in her excitement, then performed a kind of army roll under a cubicle's sickly gray desk. She lay like that for some time, balled up, observing the unruly gray cables that ran down from above. She felt safe for a few minutes and contemplated sleeping until, as was its habit, her brain moved from a feeling of being well-defended to one of being cramped and vulnerable. She slid on her belly out from under the desk and rose to a crouch.

She swung the door of that office back open and resolved to check the second floor; surely the spaces she would find there would be impregnable.

"What are you doing in here?" came a voice behind her.

She wheeled around and saw a man in a custodian's uniform peering across at her, dragging a vacuum behind him. She lurched sideways, suddenly stung by the hallway's dim light, stammered out some nonsensical excuse, then turned and ran full speed down the hall and out of the building.

She stumbled right out into a pack of students, smoking. They were laughing and joking and she knew immediately they were laughing at her. A girl was high-stepping barefoot on a short ledge overlooking the courtyard, pretending she was walking on a tightrope, arms extended out at her sides, exaggeratedly swaying back and forth, delighting her friends. Alice moved so quickly, propelled by raw instinct, that she ran right into one of the boys. He grabbed her gently in surprise; his friends looked at her with shock and concern, a dozen eyes burrowing into her at once, exposing her, leaving her secrets spilled out on clay tiles, transcribing her bank account number and learning her darkest sexual desires.

"Hey, hey, hey," the boy said softly, brown hair falling into his eyes, holding her lightly by each shoulder. He was attractive, the kind of boy she liked, angular and gangly, tall and soft. She felt moved to run her tongue down his belly and take his cock in her mouth, or perhaps to push a piece of broken glass into the soft space behind his left ear.

"Are you alright, honey?" said a tall Black girl in a miniskirt and varsity sweater.

Alice wrenched herself from the boy's loose grasp, feeling shocks of terror inside her guts, visceral and destabilizing, even deeper than what she had already felt. She ran, tearing away from them, sprinting at full bore. They called after her and she found the strength to run even faster. She crossed a wide grass quad, arcing toward the darker side to avoid being seen. She felt she could not possibly stop, but her heart threatened to explode in her chest and breathing burned her lungs. She ran for a tree then threw herself down at its base, crawling to the side to hide herself from the nearest footpath. She breathed in ragged gasps, feeling for a panicked minute that she could not catch her breath. But she laid against the tree and stared up at the sky above her through the branches of the tree, its leaves shaking lightly with the passing breeze, and soon enough she was rested, but not calmed.

The ground felt cool underneath her and her exhaustion sapped her fear. She balanced on the edge of a total loss of control, but for the moment the ceaseless acceleration of everything that was Alice, the relentless intensification of the very idea of her, brought a paradoxical calm, like how they treat hyperactivity by giving you speed. Above her the stars looked still but she knew they were wheeling their steady path across the sky. Inside her mind, dark and grandiose thoughts assaulted her without pity, whispering insistently that she was a grand being of immense power and that lying under a tree late on a cool spring night on campus she was being tracked and surveilled, her movements noted down for history and to better facilitate the campaign of stalking and disinformation that was being waged by shadowy elite forces of immense power. She did not hear voices. She never heard voices. Never in her life would she hear voices.

She was conscious, too conscious. Her self was present; it was omnipresent. She did not lose consciousness, but was bathed in it, suffocated under it, her "I" growing and growing in her perception until it threatened to blot out the world. She had never had more conscious control of her life, never. But that "I" was distended and fragile, and because it had grown so large it could not comprehend that the world was not an intricate machine designed to manipulate Alice. Paranoia had made her everything, had made her the stuff of the universe. Her consciousness drank deeply from an alien and unforgiving world.

A jolt of fear and she wobbled to her feet. She felt compelled to threaten Clara, or perhaps to warn her, but found her cellphone inoperable. She held her thumb on the button for ages, again and again, but nothing. How long ago had she last charged it? The past few days, the past week, the past month, seemed dim and unfocused to her. She remembered only taking two bottles of Adderall in six days, two bottles she had bought from an obnoxious boy she met at a party, blowing him after the sale because it felt like the thing to do, screaming at her mother when she arrived on campus unannounced, being asked to leave a class, seeing a tearful Sadie walk away from her, being held down and fucked by her hideous reeking fat stats professor and never feeling able to mouth the word "no," running a paring knife down her side and walking around campus feeling the blood ooze comfortingly down her torso, being passed around by the baseball team to access their coke, being sent a video they had taken of one of them sodomizing her over a kitchen table while the rest of them cheered and which had made the rounds all over campus, drinking to the point of blacking out, waking up in her bathroom caked in dried vomit, making the one and only piece of origami she knew how to fold repetitively until she had to tear pages out of her textbooks for fresh paper, writing and writing and writing in her notebook. For all of it she was conscious. There was no part of her mind that sought to reconcile it all with some other self. There was only this moment, this self. All of it had seemed like the thing to do.

She stumbled over her own feet, and when she caught herself she giggled at her clumsiness, and then rough hands had her and she screamed. She screamed like she hadn't screamed since she was five years old and her mother had clumsily brushed some kind of liquid bandage onto a badly scraped knee. She screamed a deep, guttural, inhuman scream, and she felt her arms pressed against her side by those of another, burly and hairy, and though she screeched and fought there was some strange comfort in being restrained.

"All right now," came an Okie accent. "All right now."

"Fuck off of me!" she screamed in utter terror, wrenching her skinny body so violently that the much larger man briefly lost his hold. She took a step toward freedom, but the other security guard grabbed hold of her, pinning her hands together in front of her as his partner regained hold of her from behind. Her wrists hurt, a twisting, wrenching hurt that made her smile.

"She's crazy on drugs," said the one in front. She thought he looked ridiculous in his dark blue uniform.

"Those aren't our fucking colors," she shouted, still twisting and kicking and shaking but unable to escape their grip. "Our colors are crimson and cream, you fucking dog."

The officer behind her grasped her wrist and pulled it behind her body. She shook with fear. Sensing that she would soon lose the opportunity, she went to spit on the officer in front of her, but at the last second felt guilty about hitting him in the face, so she redirected and spat uselessly on his nametag. Still holding her other wrist with one hand, he clicked on his shoulder-mounted radio with another.

"I'm gonna need a female down here," he said. "We need a female officer."

His radio garbled out some affirmative response. The officer behind her pulled her other hand behind her. She fought with bitter resolve, but in a moment she was clipped into handcuffs. Fully defeated, she sank to the ground and sat there, sobbing. For whatever reason, they let her.

"You're raping me," she cried in anguish. "You're raping me."

One of the officers reached delicately for her wallet; he seemed unwilling to actually put his hand in her pocket, so for a few comical seconds he grabbed at its corner until he had finally pulled it out. He rifled through it for a moment, with Alice's quiet gasps the only soundtrack. He reached again for his radio.

"She's one of ours," he said, then read her name and graduating year. He paused and waited for the indecipherable crackle back.

"They're coming," he said to his partner.

Alice sat. She regained her composure, which is to say, she regained the same level of composure she had enjoyed when running blindly through campus, chased by ghosts. The wait felt interminable. Once or twice Alice thought to run, and she gathered herself to rise and sprint away, but then her legs were leaden and walking had been rudely removed from her repertoire.

Three figures emerged from the nighttime shade under the tree, two paramedics in white and burgundy and another security guard, a woman.

The security guard grunted toward the other two, then kneeled down in front of Alice. She theatrically bent her head to the side to consider Alice's face.

"All right, sweetie," she said. "What seems to be the problem tonight?"

"They're out there," was all Alice could think to say. "I can't go anywhere. Everywhere I go, they're there."

The security guard chewed her gum. "You look tired," she said. "Real tired."

"I feel like—"

"ER," the female security guard said to one of the paramedics, who nodded. "ER?" she asked the other security guards, who shrugged their shoulders and grunted again.

"Okay, here we go," said the security guard, and she grabbed Alice by the armpit, roughly dragging her to her feet. Alice attempted to object, but no words came, and instead she let her weight drop fully from underneath her. The security guard lost her balance for a moment and swore in annoyance. One of the men grabbed her around the waist, and the two of them halfway led and halfway dragged her toward a waiting ambulance, the paramedics and remaining security guard trailing behind.

The ambulance looked menacing and alien and its flashing lights scarred the inside of her eyes.

"Okay, okay, okay," Alice said as they reached it. "I'll go. Take me in your car. I'll ride in your car please."

But the paramedics opened the back of their bus and began unfolding a stretcher. Its metal looked cold and its mechanisms were intricate and the sight of them seemed to rob Alice of her breath, and she again collapsed into a flurry of futile attempts to escape, sagging and then flexing and sagging again.

"Please, I'll ride in your car," she asked, her voice shaking. "Please, let me."

The younger paramedic could not have been much older than she was herself. He looked at her with such sadness that for a moment she thought he must know her, must have known her when she was whole and her mind was not so obviously jagged and out of step with the world that contained it. But he was only a young man who gazed upon a broken woman whose pleas were heard by no one. The security guards lifted her entirely off the ground, not hard to do, and the paramedics strapped her down to the stretcher as she convulsed.

As they rode along she periodically shook and strained against the restraints, and she scream-sobbed the whole way. The young paramedic rode in the back with her and gazed down at her mournfully, and at one point he reached his hand down as if to grasp hers, but he pulled up short and instead grasped the rigid fabric of the restraints. He made soothing noises and squeezed the restraints, like it was a hand, a baby's hand, the whole ride to the hospital.

They delicately rolled her out of the ambulance, pushed her through a set of swinging doors, and offloaded her to a pair of orderlies and a nurse, who took her into their care like longshoremen accepting a crate onto the docks. The paramedic spoke crisply to the nurse in terms Alice did not understand, cast a final sad glace at Alice's anguished face, and was gone. The nurse leaned into Alice's face and roughly pulled her right eye open grotesquely wide, peering at her pupil with the dispassion of a picky shopper searching for the perfect avocado.

"How are you, honey?"

The casually homespun nature of the question forced the paranoid center of Alice's brain to press even harder against her skull, right in between her eyes. She started to stammer out a response but choked on her words, and she shook and rattled against the restraints again.

"Looks like amphetamine psychosis," said the nurse, and Alice was pushed briskly through a set of doors into another room, a quiet dark space quite unlike the curtained-off exam rooms they had passed by. She was left there for several agonizing minutes—maybe five, maybe forty-five—left to tremble and wince and, occasionally, to scream.

Then in tromped the same nurse, a bored-looking ER psychiatrist, and an orderly. She screamed to be released. The doctor spoke softly with the nurse. He came over to Alice, still bound in restraints, and pulled her eyelids open, staring blankly from one to the other for a moment.

"Haldol," he said.

To Alice's great relief, they began to unbind her from the restraints. But they had not fully undone all of the straps when the orderly grabbed her shoulders and turned her onto her side on the stretcher. Moving quickly and without concern, the nurse pulled down Alice's sweatpants, exposing an ass cheek. She plunged a syringe into Alice's backside, then pulled her pants back up.

For a moment Alice felt and thought nothing. To her surprise, she found that they finished undoing her restraints. She felt a moment's urge to bolt, but she was gripped with the fear of when and how the medication would arrive and suddenly could not be compelled to move on her own. The orderly half-led, half-lifted Alice onto the exam room's bed, its back raised to forty-five degrees, and she leaned against it with a strange satisfaction. She had nowhere else to go, no place she'd rather be. Then the medication was upon her.

Her trapezius muscles fired, violently, frighteningly, and she was wearing her shoulders up by her ears. Her jaw twitched and her heart beat fast and staccato.

"Oh," she said, in a tone of blank and dissociative panic. "Oh."

The nurse leaned in to her, again putting a hand to her eye and staring deep into her pupils. She took her stethoscope to Alice's wrist and listened patiently.

"Are you with me honey?" she asked Alice.

But Alice was now very far away, led there by her disorder or its treatment she wouldn't have been able to say, had she even comprehended the question. She looked blankly into a spot of cool dark paint on the wall and listened to the blood flow through her skull. Her traps fired so intensely that she feared something might snap, but she had little time to luxuriate in this fear, as her mind was now overwhelmed with the comedown. It felt like every drug she had ever taken in her life, which wasn't much, was draining out of her body at the same moment. Lines of coke she had snorted years before were making their way backward through her upper respiratory tract, and three times she lifted her hand to her nose in hopes of catching physical powder. She kept wavering in and out of the moment, and at one point she realized that she was gasping involuntarily, breathing like a chubby kid forced to run circles around the soccer field. She gazed then at the face of the doctor, who stood blank and uncaring, and she found the experience of looking at him so terrifying that she fixed her eyes back on the wall.

"We're good," said the doctor, and he sped off and out of the room. The orderly shuffled out with him.

Alice was alone with the nurse. She asked her, "When do I sleep?" She felt her consciousness collapsing to a point, as though her emotional world had been dragged into a singularity arbitrarily hidden behind the wall she could not stop studying.

"It's all right honey," said the nurse. She pulled up a plastic sheet from the foot of the exam table and wrapped it around Alice's knees. A human gesture. One and done. She left the room right after. It seemed impossible to Alice that she was being left by herself, but there it was. Her neck and back muscles were no longer perpetually clamped, but they fired off and on randomly in a way that made her shake and twist on the bed. She could not believe what was happening in her brain, which was in some distant sense starting to grasp the lunacy and folly of her past few weeks, but which could not take onboard the terrible pressures of dealing with that reality. She had never felt so exposed and never would again. Her jaw seized and she somehow pulled a muscle in her tongue; the pain was sharp and strange and unexpected and it provided a few merciful moments of distraction from the storm in her mind, the feeling of being unwillingly brought back under the terrible blanket of self-knowledge.

Sleep. She must sleep. They had injected her; she was in a hospital; they had left her. She must be meant to sleep. She must. It must be coming.

She clutched the plastic blanket up around her chest and turned her cheek toward the exam bed to sleep. But sleep would not come, and with every moment her naked mind felt greater and greater pain. She must be allowed to sleep, she thought, to escape this horror, this horror of being seen by herself again. But sleep did not come. Sleep did not come. Sleep did not come.

Only after an hour of that terror was she taken, mercifully, by unconsciousness. Her last thought was to wonder who would ever find her, here, alone, deep in this place of confusion and pain. Her last sensation was the feeling of her wet cheek on a wet pillow.

Eleven

She was pissing in the utilitarian bathroom attached to her room when it first really occurred to her that she was in a mental hospital. The little room stunk of disinfectant, which annoyed her, but she reflected for a moment that it was better than the alternative, and for whatever reason this little insight pulled her into her body sufficiently for her to really consider that she had spent the past six days in a psychiatric facility.

It was a disquieting feeling, and yet "better than the alternative" was her overall impression of her current station in life. They had taken her cellphone, which was merciful; she could not bear to consider who might have sent her words of sympathy, and who might not. Her room was a double but the other bed had sat empty ever since her arrival. Ronnie, her favorite wardie—the only wardie who she had talked to at all, really—had told her every day at bed check that she would surely have a roommate the next day, but it kept not happening. The whole ward seemed strangely empty in general, and the therapist who led group had said that they were meant to have ten instead of five. Somewhere in the back of her mind Alice wondered at the efficiency of the system, poked at questions of access, but such thinking was burdensome and she did not have the means to really engage with it, so let it go.

She was taking meds daily, in the morning and before bed check. She was somewhat surprised, and even a little disappointed, that they did not force her to open her mouth to make sure she had taken her pills. But such a contrivance would have been unnecessary. Inpatient life agreed with Alice. She had taken to it immediately and without complaint. She was dedicated not to getting well but to being a good patient, which was not the same thing. When she had been there a few days and the Seroquel and lithium were slowly building up in her bloodstream she had suddenly felt confronted with the fact that she had committed to nothing, really, in the past year. She had been going to college only in the most technical sense; she had been a friend to Sadie and her rapidly shrinking social network in the most minimal sense; she had gotten fucked by sweaty men she didn't really desire and acted cold and distant toward the ones she did. Now, she found herself . . . committed. She would be the best patient this ward had yet seen.

It was early still but the pills were wending her way through her body, building up in her brain. The shot of Haldol had shaken her and her environment was destabilizing and felt unreal, but she was fairly certain that it had worn off after a day or two. The trouble was that she could not remember what normal felt like, and anyway the Seroquel and the lithium were busily working in the background to the point that she now seemed to view the world through glass, through a pane of warped and thin glass that bent everything she saw at a slight angle, and the effect was macabre and disturbing. In time this too would pass, and she was left with a dark question: Had the pills settled in, and she went back to thinking and seeing as normal? Or had she merely gotten used to the warped and bent angle, so that she now could not tell what normal even was?

Still: She excelled at being a patient as she had excelled at few other things in her unexceptional life. In the mornings that meant rising early to use the bathroom, which the addition of 1,500 milligrams of lithium salts in her diet made a bit of an adventure; waiting for morning checks, then following the crowd to the cafeteria along with the inhabitants of other wards; charbroiling stale bagels until they were somewhat palatable and brutishly cutting chunks of frozen cream cheese onto them; going to group and performing for the therapist, her peers, and herself; continuing to read the copy of *Angels & Demons* she had taken from the ward's sad library, which proceeded at a snail's pace due to her sudden and extreme memory and focus issues; lunch, sat alone like every meal, staring into her plate so that no one would attempt to talk to her, which no one ever did; one-on-ones with the psychiatrist, which were now every other day; physical activity in the rec room, like Zumba or yoga, which she enjoyed more than she would ever admit; "quiet time," in which she would read a few agonized pages at a time, or try to jot her feelings down in her journal, which had amounted to perhaps a half page in her stay there; dinner in the cafeteria, perhaps sticky and delicious spaghetti with tomato sauce and a "salad" of a few forlorn pieces of iceberg lettuce, a single cherry tomato, some slices of onion, and gloopy thick ranch dressing that reminded Alice of her mother; then evening hours, where she would sit and watch the other patients watching *Jeopardy!* or one of the judge shows or a bad TV movie. Then pills again, then lights out, then staring at the ceiling feeling the fuzz around her thoughts, then unconsciousness, deep untroubled sleep brought to her by Seroquel and by a body that had given up on fighting.

It was all terribly boring. She knew that was the point—her group therapist had said as much explicitly—and she didn't mind boring, so much. The trouble was that all of that free time inevitably left her to think about what came next, and what she had to look forward to. She was both desperate to read her outgoing texts from the past several weeks and terrified at the thought of doing so. What had been said? Who had she insulted, threatened? Did Sadie know she was in the hospital? Her parents knew, and so Sadie must. It hurt to ponder how few people were left in her life who would have been brought into this confidence. There were no longer very many who would bother to ask after her.

Her parents had driven over an hour to the facility on her first night, but they had been informed of her condition and then turned away, and for that Alice was glad. But she could not keep them at bay forever, and now the day of their first official visit had arrived. She could not imagine what she would possibly say to them.

First, though, morning check—a nurse robotically checking her pulse, blood pressure, and temperature, then meds. She had thought she would receive them from someone behind a desk, waiting in a large scrum of patients, like in the movies. She asked the nurse to give them to her so she could swallow them all at once, but she shook her head no and handed Alice her three prescriptions one at a time. The nurse asked, as she always did, if Alice was suffering from diarrhea, so Alice lied and said no. After she had left, Alice took a shower, which was operated only by a button that ran lukewarm water for exactly two minutes before needing to be pressed again; there was no temperature control. She dried herself off with four hand towels not much bigger than an unfolded napkin. Then Alice ambled down the hall to the cafeteria, again struck by the half-empty halls, and today chose a mushy but sweet fruit cup, unable to deal with the effort of applying frozen cream cheese without destroying the bagel. She finished quickly and clutched her book up to her face, simply to hide from social interaction. It was probably an unnecessary defense. Then it was time for group.

Group therapy was . . . well, it was group, comforting and alienating all at once. And strange. Alice could not, for the life of her, develop a clear or simple attitude toward it; she did not look forward to group, and did not dread it, but dreaded trying to decide if she enjoyed it. Her general commitment to being the perfect patient stood, and she would participate as asked in all things. But group . . . in years to come Alice would decide that group was a lot like travel: in hindsight, things look fulfilling and rosy that were in the actual commission of doing them rather tedious. She got little out of group in the act of going but pulled much more from it when accessing those times as fuzzy and indistinct memories. Someday she would understand the therapeutic power of hindsight.

She was, as usual, the first to arrive in the conference room. The therapist, a young woman who was clearly trying to appear older than she was, sat in her usual spot, her hair pulled into what looked like a painfully tight bun. She gave her usual half-smiling half-nod.

Soon the other four usual patients walked in. They had made their introductions every day, and Alice had tried willfully to refuse to learn their names; there was something terrifying about the prospect, about knowing them and them knowing her. But of course day after day of hearing them introduce themselves and complain about their own problems, she could not help but feel that she knew them now, at least a little. She had been told that patients would forever be cycling into and out of her group and to prepare for it, but as with her hypothetical roommate no such turnover had yet occurred. They sat quietly for a moment in their chairs, waiting a good two minutes after their session had officially started, which was one of the therapist's little contrivances.

At last she welcomed them and said that she had hoped they were having a good day. Group was an everyday thing, at least in that ward at that hospital, at least for those patients. She was unclear on why she had been put into this particular group with these particular people, and she would never learn. If she had interpreted correctly, there were two schizophrenics, one schizo-affective, one who suffered from depression and had a history of amphetamine-induced psychosis, and one Alice.

The therapist started, as she always did, with Daryl, and as always he could not be moved to introduce himself beyond correcting her—"D," he would say, "D, say D." And the therapist would immediately acquiesce and ask D to say more about himself and his day, which he would fail to do, only making soft grunting noises and occasionally stammering out a limited sentence about being hungry or cold. Always the same ritual, and every day it annoyed Alice more and more that the therapist would not simply recognize that D's name was D. D was, Ronnie had told her, a schizophrenic with negative symptoms—he was withdrawn, barely verbal, moved very little, seemed constantly to be right on the verge of falling asleep. His belly hung with meds weight, which made Alice anxious; she had not had access to a scale since they first processed her through, and saw many of the other patients were overweight, their bodies battered by the insatiable hunger their drugs infused them with. And this was in a context where they could not control their own food intake. But she was still skinny, at this point, her ribs a record of her recent velocity. In any event, D always said very little and mostly rocked back and forth in his chair, and the therapist rarely compelled him to speak given his difficulties.

"Try a papaya," she once heard him speak-singing to himself in the common room. "Try a papaya," he said, rocking gently. "Try a papaya."

He was a resident of a psychiatric hospital, seemingly a fairly long-term one, and he suffered from diabetes and hypertension thanks to his weight, but he seemed to be the closest to happy of any of them.

Jessie was not fat. Jessie was frighteningly thin. She was the depressed druggie, the one with a history of selling her body for meth and then smoking so much that she became psychotic. Alice was surprised to find that she still looked good, that she looked youthful, that her skin was not pocked with sores and her teeth were firmly implanted in her mouth. But Jessie was full of surprises. It turned out that her parents were quite wealthy and that she had attended expensive boarding schools, and it was there, not in some shady rural meth house, where she had developed her drug habit. Much of Jessie appeared on the surface to be cool, and Alice often fantasized of a life where they were tight friends. Certainly her tattoos and her profanity and her just-enough resistance to the group therapy project were attractive qualities. But there was a desperate quality to Jessie, a neediness, that kept her from ever seeming really cool. The distance between the detachment she affected and the need she clearly felt made her seem small and sad, and her petty acts of insubordination mostly just wasted time.

Today Jessie played according to the script. She said again that she felt "clinically depressed," which Alice would discover was a knee-jerk tendency within such institutions; "depressed," after all, was just a feeling. She turned over dim memories in her head of lying motionless on her dorm room floor, but found she could connect with none of it, could not make it relevant to what she was doing that day. The therapist asked Jessie if she had worked on her mood board.

"You know I have," said Jessie sullenly. "You saw me do it."

"But what did you feel, when you were doing it?"

"I felt like it was a fucking waste of time," said Jessie. She said it a little too loudly, a little too insistently, and it created the air of theatricality that attended Jessie's self-presentation as a mental patient. This was something Alice learned quickly: mental patients were competitive, and in group therapy, they would compete. Jessie clutched a pen in her hand with a grip designed to mimic holding the cigarettes she was not allowed to have. It was overplayed, undergraduate. She looked small and sick.

"Well, then, you're feeling something now, aren't you?" said the therapist, looking pleased with herself. "I hope you shared that frustration on the mood board."

Jessie's little body twitched with annoyance. It was clear she would like to fight. But fight who, and for what? In this stay and those to come Alice would find that the psychiatric hospital was a space that inspired the urge to resist but contained no solid object to resist against. It was an antagonist but not a target, a big dumb ape that moved clumsily and hurt only due to indifference and was impossible to hurt in turn, its skin too thick, its hair to shaggy, and anyway it was only a vacuous animal stumbling brutishly according to its instinct and thus impossible to hate. Jessie swallowed, loudly.

"I want out of this fucking place."

"You can leave at any time, Jessie," said the therapist, cocking her head to the side. "We've discussed this."

She clicked the plunger on her pen, in and out.

"As soon as you feel you're ready to be released to the care of your parents."

Jessie crumpled her wax paper water cup in her hand, another gesture of unconvincing theatricality.

"I'm an adult!" she shouted. "I'm fucking old enough to go on my own."

"And that's what the court order is for," said the therapist smoothly. For a moment Alice thought Jessie might break completely, but the therapist started speaking in softer tones.

"Come on, Jessie," she said. "Let's talk about food. You've been doing so well."

And so she did, and quickly the tension left the room. She talked about having a second banana yesterday to go along with her dry English muffin and black coffee, and soon enough this turned to her standard tale about the pressure her parents put on her and how getting high became her only release. As usual, by the end she was crying, as was the schizoaffective patient Cynthia, and as usual Alice wondered why she could not cry herself. The therapist once again thanked Jessie for her emotional honesty.

Cynthia went next and, as always, she told a pleasant tale about taking it one day at a time and putting one foot in front of the other. She was bright and articulate, even though she spoke only toward the ground, and she was ever-ready to acknowledge that she had a psychotic disorder. There's a certain species of mental patient, Alice would learn in time, that sees little space between recovering from addiction and managing their illnesses, and as is true in the twelve-step space they take solace in constant self-identification. Ronnie the wardie had told Alice that Cynthia was a regular presence in the hospital; she would relapse into psychosis, arrive at the facility in hysteria, be brought down with meds in a couple days, then spend the rest of the week being as compliant and receptive as she could be. She would leave all smiles and in three or four or five months return with her delusions and her conspiracy theories in thickest bloom.

Alice had sympathy for Cynthia but disliked sharing group with her because of her utter dedication to repeating self-care clichés she had found in Instagram memes. On the other hand, her introductions were usually short. The same could not be said of Gerard.

Gerard was in his mid-fifties but had a certain boyish quality to him, and had that strange feature some aging men have where his graying temples actually made him appear younger. He had schizophrenia, which produced some negative behaviors that remained permanently vague to Alice—he was paranoid about money, was the sum extent of her understanding, but she knew it must have gone beyond that for him to be here. To be here again, that is. Gerard was the type of mental patient who refused to ever drop his affected sagacious attitude, making free with a homespun folk wisdom that combined "eat pray love" aphorisms with a little bit of non-denominational Jesus and a lot of big opinions about other people's diagnoses. He had already pigeonholed Alice and chewed her ear about all of her problems, days earlier. His introduction was its usual mix of self-aggrandizement and shameless sloganeering, and the therapist's barely hidden distaste for Gerard was one of the only things Alice liked about her.

Eventually Gerard ran out of clichés and staggered to a close. "Check-ins" had once again taken half of their therapy time. With considerable ceremony the therapist rotated a whiteboard on one of those freestanding easels; it contained a word cloud, sans words. And in short order she explained that they were to share words and find connections so that they could better understand what united them. The activity went as planned, which is to say that each participant playacted their role—Jessie rolled her eyes but was eventually compelled to participate, D made soft vague noises until the therapist wrote down a word she pretended he had said, Gerard talked over everyone, Cynthia named only positive qualities in an exercise about debilitating mental illness, and Alice quietly fulfilled the requirements of the assignment, adding "scared" and "fast" and "alone" to the word cloud.

As they always did, the group ran out of steam, suppressed as they were by powerfully sedating medications and having exhausted their opportunities to talk about themselves. And so the therapist spoke soothingly and vaguely about what they had learned, running out the clock as each member of the group gradually withdrew further into their sedation and their sadness. And then group was over.

As she left to go, Alice found herself intercepted by a wardie, and she felt dull cold fear inside of her. It was time. Her parents were waiting in the visiting area.

The tables and chairs for visitors were stooped and little and her parents looked vaguely ridiculous as they waited. She walked toward them robotically until they noticed her and rose. Her father looked haggard and like he had not slept; her mother appeared beatific and calm, possessed of the maternal benevolence of one whose child was reaching out for the last branch. Alice hugged them both awkwardly; she had never shared a non-awkward hug with her father, even when she was little, but it stung to feel her mother's body pressed against her and yet so distant. They sat back down at the little table, her chair so low that her knees rose up comically high against her body.

They simply sat together, and Alice nurtured a little hope that they might just sit silently with one another for the first time in her life—exactly what she needed. But her mother soon began the expected babbling, talking about women at church, local politics, and how everyone had been asking after Alice without ever coalescing around why they might have been asking after Alice, why she had become someone that people asked after in concern. Alice's father studied the floor, as expected. Alice was only tired; her thoughts had to burrow their way through mud to get out, so she lagged behind the conversation in a way that her parents couldn't have missed. Finally her mother said something that referred to the present situation.

"They told us what you got."

Alice could only nod robotically.

"Yeah."

"They talked to you about it, right?"

The question irritated Alice no end. What did she think she was doing all day?

"Yes," she said.

"They gave me a brochure," she said, reaching into her purse. "I got you one too, so you could read it when you get out."

Alice looked at the two brochures, stamped with smiling faces on their covers, and found she could bear no ill will toward her parents. As it had periodically in recent days the fact of the burden she was imposing on her parents sent a shiver of shame down her spinal column. She thanked her mother; she could think of nothing else. Her father stirred.

"No credits, this whole past semester," he said. "I called 'em. You didn't get a single credit."

"I'm sorry," said Alice.

"They don't give you the money back," he said, then shook his head. "Goddammit, Alice."

She had not expected this—she could count the number of times her father had spoken to her in anger on one hand—but it felt good. She wanted to be castigated, needed it. She immediately regretted her reflexive apology; had she reacted angrily she might get as much as she deserved.

"I'm thousands and thousands in debt to that school," he said, shaking his head and refusing to look at her. "Thousands and thousands and no credits for an entire semester."

"I'm sorry," she said again, and felt certain she would be crying if not for the hundreds of busy little milligrams working their magic in her brain.

"We gotta, we gotta, we gotta talk," he said, now tapping his toe along with shaking his head. "When you get right."

"Talk about what?" she said, suddenly annoyed.

"You might have go to State around the corner so you can live at home," he said. "I'm breaking my back for a dorm you don't get any sleep in."

"That's not what we're here for today," said Alice's mother. Her tone had the predictable effect, and he backed off.

"Honey, we just want you to rest and get well and we'll be there for you when you get out."

"When do I get out?" asked Alice.

"Well, you're free to go whenever you're ready," she said carefully, repeating a line that Alice had heard a lot lately. "But the doctors think you need more time, and so do we."

She was not entirely unaware of the scenario—she was a legal adult, her current stretch of hospitalization was voluntary, and she could force her way out if she wanted to. She wasn't sure if she wanted to. But now her mother had let her know that they wanted her to stay, and she was sure she did not want to disobey them. Not again, and not like this.

And with that she moved back to small talk, to Alice's relief. At times her father even participated. This was a kind of ball Alice knew how to play. As she did, she turned the question of whether to stay or go over in her head again. The institution was sterile, lonely, and cold, and she was prone to feeling shame for being there. But nothing was expected of her, here, and she wanted for nothing, and she felt no particular desire to go. She felt that she was balanced on a wire between staying and going and felt that the slightest breeze could push her over onto either side and she knew if it did she would feel no remorse no matter what the direction. And here was her mother, telling her to stay awhile longer, and so that was fine by her, by her illness, and by the world.

In time they ran out of small talk and her parents rose. She clutched her mother and grasped her father's forearm in affection to ensure his own comfort. Her mother cried as she walked them to the ward door and showed them out. Alice's mouth tasted like chalk and in her head impulses rose up but could not sustain their momentum, thoughts smothered under the blanket of therapy and medication.

She wandered back to her room. She had taken to sprawling out in the empty bed during the day but Ronnie had softly told her it was unfair to the staff to force them to make another bed for no reason. Her visiting hours had gone long and she was missing origami, the only craft therapy day she had been interested in, but it didn't seem sensible to go halfway through. She picked up the Dan Brown novel and thumbed through it. She tried again to carry the thread of the conspiracy it described; shadowy figures worked tirelessly and in silence to impose the whims of ancient powers, distant and inscrutable and unseen. The words passed as easily as writing ever could, and Alice made her most aggressive advance yet, but in time she surrendered. The cognitive effects of her drugs were just too persistent. She would concentrate, and concentrate, and concentrate, and then suddenly she would be realizing that she had drifted off again. This feeling was pure hindsight—she lost time. She was reading her book and then she was realizing that time had passed in which she had not been reading her book. She read a sentence and forgot it and reread the sentence and remembered it then finished the paragraph and forgot it. So she stopped.

It was a shame. This was the perfect time to read. But her brain wanted one thing only, to rest, to reconstitute itself like vapor into a cloud or a cloud into rain. Perhaps, someday, rain into a placid

lake. Somewhere deeper in the recesses of the institution someone was screaming, but the sound was dim and distant, and then
Alice was tired in the way of high-dose antipsychotics, the wandering exhaustion that will pad into your body and settle in for a
nice long stay, and so she closed her eyes, and though it was early
afternoon she sank into a black and empty sleep.

Twelve

He was small, shorter even than Alice, but had that quintessential doctor quality of filling the room with competence and concern. He had what sounded to her like a British accent—one she took to be "posh," though what did she know of such things—but when she asked him on their first meeting he chuckled and said no, that he had been raised in Pakistan and been in the States a good twenty years. She felt sudden panic, that day, that she had said something racist, but he graciously thanked her for her interest in him and moved on.

He had seen her the first day and second and third but they were now moving to every two days, and she found it remarkable, how much she had built up in her mind that she needed to say to him, in only forty-eight hours. He started, as he always did, with discussing that morning's vitals.

"I'm still a little nervous about this blood pressure," he said, frowning into his computer screen. "If we don't get that up and stable we'll have to put you on something."

Alice was unsure of what to say.

"How are you feeling?"

She chewed on it.

"I'm all right," she said. "I'm in the bathroom a lot."

"Yes, I'm sorry," he said. "We may switch out your extended release for regular lithium. Gastrointestinal problems are very common but they often are better or worse with one or the other."

Alice had gotten used to 20-minute sessions on the toilet, where shit came out in a torrent, then in drips and drops, then in torrents again. She also had learned not to trust when she felt like she was done; her bowels, not her feelings, would have the last word.

"Eventually, we're going to start bringing you down on your lithium, from 1,500 to 1,200," he said, studying his papers. "But I want you to stay there for a while. A long while, I mean, after discharge."

"When will that be?"

"When you're ready."

"Are my parents paying for this?" she asked, possessed by a certain guilt.

"That's not my department," he said. "But at your age I imagine you'd be covered by a parent's insurance."

He hesitated.

"For now."

He leaned forward in his chair and spoke almost in a whisper.

"Do you understand what your life is going to be?" he said, with evident compassion. "Things are never going to be the same."

Alice studied the floor and considered the question. She had not really thought about her future life since she had arrived, beyond her cravings for Taco Bell and for a fumbling and sweaty sexual encounter in a car. Now he had asked her directly, and every possible future seemed absurd. The idea of returning to Norman made her very tired, but the idea of going to the local state college was an insult. Would she just drop out? Drop out into what?

"Your meds haven't fully built up in your system yet, Alice," said the doctor, rising from his chair and coming to the front of his desk. He half-sat on its corner. She got the feeling he had done that many times before.

"The side effects will prove in time to be punishing," he said. "You need to be prepared for the weight gain, emotionally. You need to be prepared for the bathroom issues to continue. You need to be ready for akathisia, for it to embarrass you in public, to wake you up in the middle of the night. You need to commit to taking your medication, every day, or you will get sick again."

"For how long?"

He nodded with pursed lips.

"Some people do grow out of it," he said. "But not until their fifties or sixties or later. And for some, I'm afraid, the condition is degenerative."

He wandered over to the window. It was a precious piece of real estate in the facility; her room had no windows and the group therapy room had no windows and the cafeteria's windows were set far back against one wall, and when she arrived to eat, all the seats down there were always already taken. But she felt no desire to gaze.

"That's not our immediate concern," he said. "We need to set you up for success. It's essential that you find an experienced out-patient psychiatrist who you can see regularly. Twice weekly, at least, to start with."

"I don't know if there are a lot of psychiatrists in my home-town," she said.

"There are in Norman," he said. "Aren't you going back to school?"

"Not for a while," she said. Nothing had been decided, but she knew.

"Ah," said the doctor, wandering back to his perch on the desk. He tilted his head to the side, but still she would not make eye contact.

"Do you understand, Alice?" he said softly.

"I think so," she said. "I need to take meds, I need to do therapy."

He waited an extra beat, seemingly hoping for a little more, then reached down and gently took Alice's hand, which he clutched delicately like a Fabergé egg. It surprised her but did not scare or offend her, and for a moment she lived with the quiet glory of human touch. His hand was small and soft like a woman's, but there was something paternal and solid about it.

"You have a psychiatric disorder, Alice, and we will treat it with psychiatry," said the psychiatrist. "The etiology of your condition is not well understood, but for those who stay on their medication, the prognosis is good. For those who don't, it isn't. Do you understand?"

"Yeah."

He released a slight soft humming sigh, the closest thing to a sign of anything other than total restraint she would ever observe in him. He nodded slightly to bring a brief internal conversation with himself to a close.

"There are forces raging inside of you, Alice," he said. "Forces that you can't control or comprehend. Their battle inside of you provoked your recent episode. And they're still fighting, even now, even as you sit inside of my office. The medications suppress them but can never kill them. And if you let them they will come back to the forefront of your mind and you will rage and riot again. They are testing the fence, Alice, even now. You must think of your pills like armor for the battle that your psyche will fight every day of your life for decades to come. And I think it would be good, healthy even, if you worked up a little fear. Learn to fear those forces. Know what they are. You must understand that they are intent on ruining your life and then killing you, Alice, they want to provoke you, to force you to burn down every relationship you ever had that ever meant anything to you, and then they will try to provoke your suicide. The only time they will cease whispering into your ears is when they decide to scream instead. Do you understand, Alice? Do you understand your enemy? Do you see him for what he is, in all his destruction? Are you prepared to fight?"

"Yes," said Alice.

"Good," he said, straightening up and heading back behind his desk, where he again rustled his papers, as if to bookend his warning. For once, Alice was not annoyed by a doctor's routines. Perhaps she was even grateful.

"Do let me know about the diarrhea, and then we'll see about switching the lithium," he said. The session was over.

Alice rose to go. She stole a glance back at the green outside. She stopped as she reached the door.

"Do I look tired?" she asked.

He kept studying his papers for a moment, seeming not to hear her, then gave her the briefest glance.

"No," he said. "You don't look tired at all."

Back in her room, Alice slept, dreaming of antique gods of mercy, or maybe of cheese fries at the diner.

Thirteen

Alice did, in fact, spend the rest of her college education at State nearby, and she did, in fact, live at home the whole time. She lived the life of a commuter student, keeping her head down, making no friends, occasionally waiting for professors after class to resolve some sort of problem with macroeconomics or algebra. She took a major in marketing; she could not think of a reason not to. Boys sometimes approached her but she could not bear to see them away from campus. There was something about other students that reminded her of all she had given up in coming there, that she would never be a college student again, not really, not in the only way that mattered. She took a townie for a boyfriend, a dumb sweet thick gentle boy named Scott who was unobjectionable and had his own apartment. The first time she slept over at his place her father raised hell, until her mother quietly reminded him that she had slept wherever she liked in Norman.

Alice did in fact find an outpatient psychiatrist, though it wasn't easy, and she did in fact comply, and surprisingly that was. She had fruitlessly searched and searched on the website of her father's insurance and could find nothing nearby. She was amazed to find that there was not a single practicing psychiatrist in her hometown, and only a couple in the towns surrounding, neither of whom were accepting patients or expecting to anytime soon. And so she was forced to drive an hour each way, twice a week at first, to see her doctor. He was old and white-haired and absentminded, and he treated her with distraction and kindness, both of which were precious to her. She got up every morning and took the pills and she took them before she went to bed. For months after she moved home her mother hovered in the bathroom behind her while she took her meds, until finally Alice had to ask her to stop.

She grew fat around the middle and could not shake it, not with the StairMaster or with intermittent fasting or with keto. She would go long days where it didn't bother her and then without warning her hatred of her own body would assault her and she would cry and cry and her mother or dear Sadie would stroke her hair. There was no escaping the weight gain, only arresting it, perhaps, and even then it would be stuck in a place that left her breathless and unattractive. She did still get checked out by boys, and she did at times feel admiration for herself. But behind the weight lay the terrible understanding that her body was no longer her own, that some alien force exerted control over her size, over the very matter that constituted her self.

She had taken to shunning social media; she could not bear to see the lives of her friends, at Norman or other schools, who appeared from the distance of a smartphone to be living the collegiate lives of her dreams. She found that when she was not actively thinking of what she had left behind and would always miss, she was more or less happy. More, because she actually fit into her new life well, a life of quiet nights spent alone in her room, studying in the public library where she had spent so many hours as a child, and sitting on her boyfriend's couch watching *The Office*, never talking, which was both her preference and his. Less, because she was taking a mood stabilizer, an antipsychotic, an anticonvulsant, two antidepressants, and occasionally an anxiolytic. Happy or not was hard to tell.

Now she was approaching the end of her college career, and her mother was making more and more noise about her finding a career. Her father said nothing but his influence was palpable. She had not said that they would cut Alice off, and they would probably never do so clumsily or in total, but the message was plain enough, and she was aware that she had been drinking heavily from their generosity for years.

She was ready to start making some money and eager for her own apartment; the warmth of moving back in with her parents had faded long ago, and she had no interest in moving in with Scott, who she liked well enough and kept at an arm's distance and who never complained. But she was filled with apprehension about finding a job. She had no ambition, no internal sense of a desire to be productive or to make money. This was an advantage in that there were few restrictions on the jobs she would accept but a disadvantage in that there were few reasons for any particular employer to hire her. She longed only for a simple email job, preferably remote, or else where she would have her own quiet corner cubicle so that her coworkers could easily forget her existence.

Part of her worries lay in her scattered and fickle mind. The antipsychotics that had thickened her thighs had also thickened her mind. Thinking on Seroquel felt like trying to run through waist-deep water. Pushing thoughts through the avenues and gullies of her brain felt like physical effort, felt like it made her brain lose its breath. She was beset with distractibility, totally unable to concentrate during lectures, forcing her to constantly tear her attention back to what was happening in front of her only to discover once again that her mind had drifted despite all of her efforts. Memory too had become a site of aerobic exercise, and she shuffled through the file cabinet of her memories with thumbs that were thick and sore. She grew used to opening up tabs in her web browser only to forget what she had intended to do with them by the time she went to tap in a URL; she had given up on ever again remembering what show she wanted to watch, what song she wanted to listen to.

Today she was blindly clicking around a jobs website and seeing the same dross that she always saw, multilevel marketing schemes (scam), part-time stocker at Aldi (wages too low to move out), warehouse worker (soul-destroying), TikTok content creator for an insurance company (low-paying, soul-destroying, and probably a scam). She didn't feel that her ambitions were unrealistic;

she was looking only for a bullshit white collar-adjacent low-level admin job, something where she could hide in her cubicle all day and fill in spreadsheets and bring in homemade cookies to make people like her. The idea of a job she actually enjoyed or would feel proud of doing was quite alien to her and the rare times when it entered her mind she shook it right off. The concept of ambition seemed even more distant than her emotions, these days, and as fickle as her memory.

Scott had offered, lately insistently, for her to move in with him, always sold as a means to save on rent. She liked her boyfriend but the idea horrified her and his sense that this was a reasonable thing to want made her wonder if the relationship had run its course. Scott was big and amiable and chubby in that good boy way, and he plainly loved her in an uncomplicated manner that he would never question. He was as comfortable as her favorite hoodie and he asked very little of her, acted blasé when she told him about her condition and her medications, and drove her everywhere she asked even though living with her parents provided her with a car. In many ways he was the perfect partner for where she was in her life. The only trouble was that he wanted, as most people do, for their relationship to progress. He wanted them to get serious. Unfortunately for both of them, the serious truth was that she did not love him and knew she never would, and every time he pushed her to get closer he brought them closer to a break up.

He had his quirks. He almost never drank more than two beers a night, saying that he wanted to stay ready to drive, even when they were relaxing at home and would soon go to bed. But a couple times a year he would go out with his friends and come home absolutely wasted, belligerent, demanding anal sex. He never crossed the line into abuse but simply became a different kind of boyfriend. Alice always acquiesced, in part because acquiescing was all she was good at but also because drunk and demanding Scott was hotter than regular Scott, and being sodomized by a drunken meathead reminded her of her very favorite times at college. When sober his tastes were quite the opposite; he had taken to asking her to call herself a slut while they were having sex, and then to describe slutty behavior from the past, of which she had a rich archive to draw from. Once he had come, he would sometimes ask her in worried tones if she had actually done those things, but she would lie and reassure him that she could never. It sometimes made her miss the old days, but the pills had sufficiently curbed her obsessive desire to be used and degraded by men who had contempt for her. Lately she had been trying to take a mental inventory of what she really wanted and what her disorder wanted, and she had come to the conclusion that when of sound mind she was just a moderately-horny young woman who, in the right situation, would rather do the slutty thing than to send a boy home disappointed, however that might sound to progressive ears. She didn't love Scott's fantasy game, the slut game, but nor did she hate it. All she really wanted was to be asked for something and to give in. And she wished he would take what he wanted a little more often, take a little more without asking.

And suddenly she realized that she was not searching for jobs and had not been for a long moment. To become distracted while performing a repetitive and unpleasant task was of course simply to be human. But with the antipsychotics there was something different. The assault on her focus was totalizing, inescapable. She spared a moment to feel sorry for herself about it, and then found herself wondering whether she hadn't just been thinking about the same exact subject moments before. Her memory difficulties colluded with her focus problems; they were co-conspirators.

She was gripped with the sudden gastrointestinal issues that were but one of lithium's little gifts. She raced to the bathroom and evacuated her bowels. Shit exploded out of her at first, then paused as she felt her stomach churn, and then shot out in brief ropes again and again. She flushed continuously, the only thing that made her feel like she had a sense of agency when her body was once again asserting its dominance over her. When it felt like she was done, she did not rise, as she had quickly learned not to trust that feeling. And, indeed, after several minutes she started going again.

When she was done she meticulously washed her hands, like a surgeon scrubbing in for the operating room. She sweated in the air-conditioned house. She went back to her laptop but felt such overpowering exhaustion at the thought of job hunting that she simply closed its lid. She sat on the edge of the bed and attempted to decide how she felt.

This was less abstract than it sounds. Under the weight of so much medication, trying to deduce her own emotional state was like grasping around for a dropped object in the dark; even after you find the thing, you have to feel its shape for a moment before you're confident you know what it is. Her first priority was more prosaic—she had to decide if she was well and truly done having to shit or if she would have to head back to the toilet in twenty minutes. This was a ritual for her, one that impacted her basic freedom to take the car out and leave the house without fear of suddenly needing a bathroom. She determined that she was safe, for now. She lifted her hand to study it for shakes; there was none. At times the lithium made her hands shake to the point where she could not safely lift a coffee cup to her lips, but this was thankfully rare. So was the akathisia, a vestige of the antipsychotics; the doctors called it psychomotor restlessness, a repetitive twitch in her extremities that was sometimes quite violent in the rare occasions that it afflicted her. She had woken up Scott in the middle of the night a half-dozen times thanks to powerful spasms in her legs. He would simply wake her up to comfort her, without anger.

When Sadie asked her what exactly was lacking in Scott, Alice would grow vague, dissemble. She could not put it into words herself. She was aware that she was holding him to an impossible standard; he did not make her feel the way she felt when her body was made of electricity and she walked naked under the light of a stark and friendly moon.

What did she actually want? It was not quite the same question as how she really felt, nor did answering it follow the same process. Trying to catalog her desires felt like going on tiptoes and peeking over a fence to follow a baseball game—the action was there, that was undeniable, but to observe it required the constant application of attention and felt physically tiring. And being with Scott relieved her of that burden. She did not need to ask what she really wanted in and from a man because sweet boring dependable Scott was in the way. This was a blessing. What other blessings did she have to count? Well: She was not choking with emotions she could not begin to express anymore. Focusing on any one thing felt like trying to shoot a target that kept skittering away, but her mind was also uncluttered, free of insistent intrusive inexplicable thoughts. There was no pain. That was clear enough.

When she first got out she had spent long hours watching videos from the "anti-psychiatry" movement, morbidly fascinated, disturbed and intrigued. She watched video after video where people decried their past psychiatric treatment, declared mental illness to be a psyop designed to enforce social norms, and described the poisonous effects of the drugs that were no longer coursing through their systems. Hollow-eyed young women stared straight into the camera and described the awful collusion between their parents and their psychiatrists, the forced hospitalization, and most of all the narcotizing medications that made them loose and pliable.

The videos had something like the opposite of their intended effect; they left Alice comforted. Perhaps it was the assurance that the drugs really were doing something, that she had been affected in more ways than weight gain, night sweats, shivering hands. Perhaps it was her contrarian streak. Or perhaps the videos just made a lonely young woman feel like a part of a community.

Some of the anti-psychiatry types spoke out against "medication spellbinding," a condition (they claimed) that caused those using psychiatric medications to love their drugs despite all of their downsides. How this differed from simply being happy that medication was working was unclear. Did she love her medications? She couldn't say. They were now all worked into her system, and the bimonthly blood tests that the hospital insisted on showed her lithium and olanzapine levels were in the correct range, the "therapeutic" range. But how did she feel? She felt that the drugs were people, that they had character, personalities. She could not of course decompose the effect of so much medication down to the individual pills, had no way to tell the mood stabilizer from the antipsychotic from the anticonvulsant from the antidepressant. But she had deep intuitions about them and the way they interacted in her system, interacted socially, like hot-tempered roommates in the shabby apartment of her brain.

Lithium caused her innumerable problems, but now it was an old friend, a sweet quiet voice of calm and composure, always present but never insistent. Yes, it had softened her body, but also her mind. She had dated a boy briefly at OU who was obsessive about his guitar pedals—sadly for him, the obsession was greater than his talent—and he had once explained to her what each one did. It was the sort of thing girls were expected to suffer through, but she was fascinated; there were so many of them, and they all had their own special function, and the boy explained them all with reverence and enthusiasm. She recalled him describing the compressor lovingly.

"A compressor filters out the bottom and the top of your tone," he said, fondling the heavy metal casing as he spoke. "You take out the bottom range and you take out the top and what's left has a much more forceful attack."

He had gone on to tell her about phasers and flangers and envelope filters and more. It was, sadly, the peak of their relationship, but he was one of very few boys who she was on good terms with after they ended things.

She rolled that conversation over in her mind when the lithium built up in her system over the course of weeks. She could not say that she now had a more forceful attack, on lithium; nothing she had done since she moved back in with her parents could be called forceful. But it was the perfect metaphor nevertheless. Lithium filtered out the bottom and the top, the high and the low. Whether there was enough left to feel in the middle for her to remain human was not a question she could answer, not now, perhaps not ever. No one could do as much Googling as Alice had done and not come across the accusation that high-dose lithium obliterated emotions. Whether that was true was impossible for her to answer. There was no thermometer in her limbic system; the highs and lows within the range she could feel appeared real to her. It was true that she could not remember the last time she had felt joy, but then there had been no joy when she was lying in the fetal position on her carpet or when she obsessively tracked the former friends she knew had betrayed her on Instagram. Lithium was a friend. For now.

Olanzapine . . . She had once seen a *Law & Order* episode where the accused, a schizophrenic, had described the side effects of his antipsychotic meds. He compared thinking under their influence to "pawing through a wool blanket." For her it felt like swimming through mud. The drugs were remarkable at their intended purpose; that shot of Haldol had been a singular experience, a life-changing one, the experience of all of her attention collapsing into a single point while her muscles spasmed uncontrollably. It had not been pleasant or unpleasant. It had simply *been*, an experience unmoored from any definition of pain or pleasure. Besides, she had not followed her diseased mind down dark alleys of paranoia and delusion since. But treating her condition with antipsychotics was like soaking an entire city to put out a fire on one street, like wrapping an entire child in duct tape to prevent bruises and scrapes. Olanzapine was indiscriminate, indifferent. It made her fatigued, it toyed with her focus, it shattered her memories as they were being made. Mercifully, it also put her into a deep sleep, every night, a coma on demand.

Lamictal, that was her enemy. It was a drug first intended for epileptics, and in their online forums many spoke of the drug with horror stories. There was something buzzy about it, an all-encompassing scratchiness, a jumping-out-of-her-skin feeling. She had developed a rash because of the Lamictal, which was a matter of considerable anxiety given that the drug could cause rashes that were fatal. (The concept of a fatal rash, in and of itself, made Alice want to head for the hills.) A panicky trip to the dermatologist led to good news—yes, she was on Lamictal, and yes, it had given her a rash, but it was not the bad rash, the killer rash. She had left with a prescription for a big jar of gloopy ointment that eventually cured it. Scott's fundamental pliability was put to good use as Alice ordered him to apply it on her harder-to-reach areas. Rash or not, she hated the drug, and repeatedly asked her psychiatrist to drop it. He was a kind and distant man who she now mostly saw by phone, and he told her that he was unwilling to "upset the apple cart" given her progress. She blamed everything on the Lamictal from then on, the vague and transient symptoms, the headaches, the blurred vision.

The bupropion, well, it was hard to say. It gave her a little kick in the morning, which she appreciated, and had been delighted to find that it could result in weight loss, though it had done little to arrest her own weight gain. It was an antidepressant, and she had not been depressed, and that was enough for her to value those easily-swallowed white pills. The fluoxetine was similar—she was rarely horny but was never depressed. The pink Xanax sometimes enticed her, and she had on occasion taken twice the prescribed dose to relax, but she mostly worked the program and avoided it. The Xanax was not so much for anxiety or tension but rather a hedge in case her brain got too fast again; if she felt the paranoia settling in, she was to take a couple and call her shrink immediately. Rounding out her medicine cabinet were big thick horse pills of trazodone, for sleep, but she was sleeping fine without them and the handful of times she had used them she had endured an awful druggy hangover the next morning. And those were the stations of the cross at the church of her recovery.

Then she stared into her full-length mirror, saw that softening belly, those ever-expanding thighs, the layer of fat growing around her jowls, and all good things in the world suddenly died, and she was tempted to pour all the pills down the sink.

Instead, she went and sat on the toilet for five more minutes, without progress. Satisfied that she would not suddenly have to use the bathroom on the twenty-five-minute drive to Scott's apartment, she slipped out and into the truck and away from home. Alice's mother had given up on keeping track of her movements, and anyway, she liked Scott, which was another point against him.

Alice arrived to find the apartment empty, as she had expected. She let herself in with the keys he had insisted on giving her. He was still at work, a decent landscaping job that had no chance for advancement but held the promise of him starting his own business someday, tearing out stumps and mowing lawns. Alice knew from her mother that the owners of such businesses could clear into the six figures for themselves, once they were established, and anyway she liked that Scott worked with his hands. For now, she luxuriated in the quiet and solitude. She had never really experienced real loneliness, not when she was in her right mind, and she enjoyed trying it on for size. She climbed into bed and stared at the ceiling, occasionally checking her phone, occasionally dozing.

Hours later, Scott came home. He looked how he always looked—dumb, thick, and kind. He lay next to her in bed and, with his typical subtlety, ground his crotch into her leg. She had no interest in sex, so she dutifully unzipped his pants and jacked him off. Eventually he groaned and just as he did she leaned down and let him come in her mouth, and the groan and the feeling made her horny, just exactly at the moment that he stopped being able to fuck her. Some dim memory flitted through her head of scandalous high-risk sex from the past, the kind she knew in a clinical way she should regret, but never could. It made her hornier, and she knew the story would make Scott horny as well, but the moment had passed; he had used her hand and mouth to jack himself off, and now he would be docile and compliant and not bother her with talk of love and commitment. Later that evening she went into the bathroom, ostensibly to take a shower, and masturbated sitting on the toilet, thinking of the debased behaviors she now could only remember and would never again think to take part in. It was the one and only aspect of her episodes that she would ever romanticize. Either way, she found that she couldn't come.

She lay next to Scott while he watched *The Office*, reading inspirational Instagram memes. She had done a purge of her follows recently of everyone she knew at OU, as self-defense against bad feelings. She opened her notes app and reread, for the hundredth time, the apology letter she had written for Clara. She hadn't talked to Clara in a long time, and there were others that she had more immediate reason to apologize to, but Clara haunted her. She felt desperate to make restitution, to make things right. But the email was long and meandering in that way that makes people think you're crazy, and that was the opposite of its intent. It would take months before she had whittled the email down to the brute basics and, she hoped, into a tone that seemed appropriately formal without being weird.

The email read:

Dear Clara,

I have wanted to write to you so many times, but I've never known quite what to say. I do know the most important part: I'm sorry. I'm so sorry you had to go through all of that with me when all you ever tried to do was be a good roommate and friend. I was told you heard about my episode and my hospitalization. I'm months into recovery. I'm stable and happy. And I just need you to know that I wasn't myself, when all of that happened . . . You were someone I thought would be a lifelong friend, but you met me at the worst possible time. I'm sorry I hurt you. I'm sorry I violated so many of your boundaries. I don't expect you to ever have me for a friend again, but I'm sorry, and I miss you.

Yours truly,

Alice

Clara never replied. They would run into each other years later and exchange pleasantries but would never reconnect in any real way. Clara was the first on Alice's list of friends forever lost to her disorder. But not the last.

Fourteen

It took two more years of looking, but she eventually found her inoffensive office job. It required a move to Oklahoma City. Alice was of two minds about the change. To her, Oklahoma City seemed as vast and frightening and unknowable as Tokyo. But it was far enough away that her parents wouldn't feel emboldened to just drop by, and, she hoped, far enough away that it would provide an excuse for her to gently set Scott free. Sadly, he responded to the news of her move with his usual implacable calm, and proceeded to talk about how they could take turns visiting on weekends. Alice hung there for a moment, silent, well aware that this was the moment to rip off the Band-Aid and cut him loose, but found she could not do so. He was just too dim and sweet. Besides, she needed someone to help move her into her apartment.

Her parents cosigned on her lease; she was still digging out from her extravagant credit card spending when she was unwell. It was a spare studio apartment in a drab building, but it had everything she needed—her own little space, quiet, neighbors who kept their heads down, and plenty of parking. There was a semi-convenient bus line and she had planned on taking it regularly, to save on gas and give her time to read, but within two months of starting the job she was driving at least four days a week. The lure of the car was just too great.

She liked Oklahoma City alright. Its central position in the state meant that nowhere else in Oklahoma was too far away, not that she ever went anywhere but home. It was a million-plus metro and thus allowed for variety in food and culture; it also lent her new endeavors a certain kind of cachet in the rare event that she ever reconnected with friends from school. But it was also a modestly sized city by more extravagant standards, fewer than 700,000 people within the municipal borders, and for some reason this comforted her. She knew that she was not, and would never be, a New York or LA sort of girl. That was okay. She had watched Sadie slowly descend into the sadness of someone whose big city dreams were not coming true.

Her building was a squat two-story job in a larger apartment complex. She would have preferred to be on the second floor, but had lucked into a corner apartment, so she got more windows and had no neighbors to the east; she dutifully put her Bluetooth stereo into the rear east corner of her apartment so that she could listen to music without disturbing those around her. Her neighbors above were a family of mixed Native and Hispanic descent, or so she guessed. Their children could be loud at night, but their endless laughter always brightened her mood, and the patter of feet above gave her the feelings of having a big family with many siblings that she had been denied as an only child. Her neighbor to the west was an older gentleman with a severe face and oversized glasses. She only caught glimpses of him when he would roam the parking lot at night, chain-smoking cigarettes.

She had now been living and working in Oklahoma City for six months, which was more than enough time to grow to love the place, then slowly grow to resent it. But perhaps that resentment was only an epiphenomenon of her profound unhappiness at work.

She pulled into her designated space, far from the door. She clutched her worn overlarge purse and an iced coffee as she hurried through the revolving door. She had taken her old college backpack into work every day, until a female colleague admonished her that no one would take her seriously if she kept bringing a backpack to work. So she spent two hundred and fifty dollars she couldn't afford to waste on a sharp leather briefcase. The consequence was, unfortunately, even worse; the boys club in her office howled with laughter at a twenty-five-year-old woman, at the bottom of the corporate totem pole, bringing a briefcase to work. Even the woman who had told her to ditch the backpack rolled her eyes at Alice. She told her immediate supervisor she felt sick and went home two hours into her workday, then bawled as she made her commute home. The purse, battered though it was, would suffice.

She sneaked into her little gray cubicle. She sighed and turned on the nondescript Dell desktop. For whatever reason, she was required to do most of her work on the company's computer; her laptop was only allowed for certain tasks, though she much preferred to use it. She was, at least, allowed to use a network drive shared between both.

She sucked down the last of her iced coffee and checked her cellphone. Her morning tasks were all spreadsheet entries. It was laborious but thoughtless, and indeed she was paid like someone whose work was thoughtless. Her finances just worked out if she spent absolutely nothing beyond her rent and essential expenses. She had been forced to "borrow" money from Scott to pay for various wants and needs, and his repeated requests that they move in together were looking more and more like a practical necessity.

She spent over an hour alternating between staring into the spreadsheet and staring into her phone. Luckily, her supervisors had little grasp on how long the tasks she needed to complete would actually take and consistently overestimated. She knew them well enough now to know that this was not a product of kindness, but she still happily took the credit she was receiving for getting everything done by deadline. And she needed that credit; she got credit for precious little else.

Her antipsychotic medication made her a bad employee. She zoned out in meeting after meeting. She would say to herself, "Pay attention, pay attention, pay attention," and then she found that time had passed, time was gone, and she had not noticed it. Usually this just meant that she didn't know what had been said, but often enough one of the bosses caught and reprimanded her.

Her memory flagged and failed her, particularly later in the day. She spent far too many moments wondering which was worse, asking her boss to tell her again what he'd already told her to do, or doing the wrong thing. She often managed to do both.

She intended to disclose her disability to the HR department when she started work, but in typical fashion had put it off for a couple weeks. And in those couple weeks she had absorbed enough about her workplace culture to know: if she told anyone in the company about her disability, everyone in the company would know. Whatever the HR person told her about anonymity would be a lie. She disliked her boss, and she despised her boss's boss, a leering and casually cruel man. She could not bear to let them know her condition. But this left her with no excuse as her focus and memory failed her again and again.

"You're gonna be late to your meeting," said another employee, one of the few other women. It was not said with affection, as nothing she said to Alice was, but it was a favor nonetheless. Alice grabbed her notebook and a pen and hurried down the hall.

She didn't know what this meeting was about, as usual, but it didn't matter much; she had never understood why she was required at these meetings anyway. There were perhaps three of these almost-daily meetings where she had actually had something to contribute, in her entire time there. Sometimes she was asked to take notes, which bothered and frightened her. Bothered, because several secretaries would inevitably sit in, and they were presumably the ones who should have been taking notes. Frightened, because notetaking provided evidence of her problems following meetings. But she dutifully turned in her notes to her boss and he robotically thanked her, and never once had anyone mentioned one of the many missed elements in the notes. Like so much else in that job, it seemed that she was taking the notes just to take them.

She sat down in the corner and tried to look small. It didn't work.

"It's the sky-blue blouse today," said her boss's boss as he walked into the conference room. A couple of the other senior employees chuckled. This was a more or less daily part of the ritual at work. He never commented on her body, only her clothes or bag, maybe her hair if she'd recently had it cut. It was always embedded with a kind of forced jocularity, a surface we're-all-friends-here vibe that would have made any complaining about it look forced and foolish. But there was never any doubt that there was menace in every word he said to her.

She thought back to every teacher and professor and boss in her life who had treated her the same way, the friendly disdain, the predatory kindness, waiting for the other shoe to drop.

"Alice," said her boss. The meeting had begun. She had been staring off into the distance. She mumbled out a strangled apology and rededicated herself to her notes. The meeting was one of those where at no point did the actual product and services provided by her company enter the discussion. It was pure managerialism, KPIs and action items and communication avenues and synergy. Among other things, this made her notes useless, even when she was able to bear down and take them; the inevitable output was a diagram linking abstractions to other abstractions.

She tried to think her way through what her office actually did and how it made money, and then attempted to imagine a way in which she might be essential to that process. She knew that they were buying debt, of some kind, or perhaps it was risk. They definitely bought and sold something intangible, some abstraction of pure capitalism that Alice could not understand.

"Alice, are you with us?" said her boss, not attempting to hide his annoyance. Someone else at the table snickered.

"I'm sorry," she said, and began scribbling in her notes.

"I asked you a question," her boss said.

"I'm sorry," she said again. "Yes, I'm with you. With us."

"Really?" he said. "Because it sure looks like you'd prefer to be anywhere else but here."

"Okay, okay," said her boss's boss. "We're all family here." And he winked at Alice.

She struggled through the rest of the meeting, avoiding further embarrassment. As she packed up her stuff to return to her cubicle, her boss came and leaned against the table near her. He didn't even wait for everyone else to leave the room before he reprimanded her.

"I've been noticing your problem with focusing on your work, Alice," he said, speaking in a measured and composed tone. "And we've already talked about your memory."

"I know, sir, I'm sorry," she said. Then she gathered herself and, fearing for her job, attempted to go for it. Much more of this and her reputation at work wouldn't matter because she wouldn't have a job.

"You know, I haven't told you this before, but I'm on medication that, uh—"

"What kind of medication?" he said. His tone was predatory. She stole a glance out of the window and then looked back at him. She clocked him then as she had clocked him the very first day: He was a man who would spare no compassion for a woman struggling with her condition, and would likely find a way to fire her if she admitted to it. Or, worse, to let her wriggle for weeks or months on a pin.

"It's, um, allergy medicine," she said. "It makes me groggy and—"

"There are a lot of people on allergy medication working here, Alice," he said. "You're the only one telling me she can't focus on her work because of it."

She looked down at her feet and nodded.

"I'm sorry, sir," she said.

"There are a lot of people who would love your job," he said, crossing his arms in front of him in an affected casual manner. "Do you value your job?"

"Of course I do, sir."

"Then act like it," he said, turning to go. "You're on thin ice."

And with that, he turned and stalked off. She walked back to her cubicle with her head down and rushed through eating her lunch. While she was halfway through her salad her boss's boss padded toward her. She half-stood and then sat back down when he approached.

"Don't worry about it," he said, with an unconvincing chuckle. "We all eat our shit around here. You'll be fine."

"Thank you, sir," she said. He crept closer to her; his crotch was perhaps six inches from her face.

"Listen, some of us are going to the bar after work," he said, leaning against the desk built into her cubicle. "Why don't you come?"

He loomed over her. She wished she had just stayed standing when he came over, but it would feel too weird to stand up now.

"Oh, I don't know," she said. "My boyfriend . . ."

Perhaps if she had finished her sentence she would have been spared. Perhaps. But trailing off in this way gave him the only opening he needed.

"Aw, come on," he said. "Invite him along. You have to come. We're all family here."

At that, he reached down and grasped hold of her wrist lightly. He didn't pull it anywhere. He just held it.

"I think it's a good idea for you to come."

And so she said yes, though she dreaded the idea. She was at least a little comforted by the fact that he had said Scott should come. He wouldn't, of course; it would be a long drive, and anyway Scott never did anything after work, nothing but video games and Netflix.

The rest of the day passed quickly, which was strange, because spreadsheet entry and emails never went quickly. She entertained the notion of slipping out of the building unseen, but when she emerged into the parking lot her boss's boss and two coworkers, one older and one younger, were waiting for her.

"Uh, are other people coming?" asked Alice.

"Just the four of us!" said her boss's boss. Alice's heart sank further.

"We're going to the bar at Chili's."

"All right, I'll follow you," said Alice.

"No need," her boss's boss said, walking up to her and putting his arm around her hip. "You can ride with me."

"Oh, no," said Alice, pulling away from his grasp. "I may want to leave early."

"Oh, don't worry," he said, gesturing toward his Mercedes in its choice spot in the parking lot. "I'll take you home whenever."

"Well, we have to come back here to get my car," she said, but now he was grasping her wrist and pulling her along to his car. She took one last forlorn look at her own car and climbed in. She consoled herself that she could always get an Uber back.

The drive was unbearably awkward for her, but blessedly short. He asked her basic getting-to-know-you questions about college and where she grew up. When they got out at Chili's, she grew anxious as she realized that they had beaten the others to the restaurant.

"Come on, let's grab a table," he said to her.

To her relief, the younger coworker showed up right then, and the older slightly after.

They got a small booth table near the bar. The bric-a-brac of American casual dining hung on the walls around them. Her boss's boss and his older colleague laughed and joked, talked about sports, tried to banter with the waitress, drank whiskey. Alice drank a sickeningly sweet blue cocktail and thereafter declined the many efforts to buy her another drink. Her only comfort was that the younger coworker, seated next to her, looked as uncomfortable as she did. He mutely sipped a single Bud Light.

"Well, I should head home," she said. "I'll just grab an Uber."

"I'll drop you off at work," said the younger coworker, seizing the opportunity to go.

"Nonsense," said her boss's boss. "We're just getting started. Both of you."

Again, the jocular menace, the friendly coercion. And then he punctuated it.

"Switch seats with me," he said to the younger colleague.

The younger man looked stricken, taken aback; Alice herself couldn't muster a word. This demand was so nakedly aggressive that she lacked a sense of how to respond. Her shocked coworker rose and Alice found herself hemmed into a booth with a large and sweaty man sitting too close to her.

Casually, he reached his hand around her waist, clutching her thigh. Again she wanted to scream but felt she couldn't. Lodged in her brain was the thought that something was so deeply wrong here that someone or something would be obligated to come along and put an end to it. But it just kept on going.

As time dragged on her boss's boss and his buddy got drunker. Gradually the hand on her thigh migrated up to her breast. She jumped a little in her seat and swatted at his hand. This apparently amused him, and he chuckled as he withdrew his hand. Shortly after, he was again clutching her breast.

When he got up to go to the bar, she knew she had to escape. She jumped up, figuring that he would take a few moments to buy his drink, but he was wasted enough to be beyond propriety and was watching out of the corner of his eye, ready to lunge.

He went for her, then, pulling her so close her head was pressed against his flabby chest. She struggled and pushed but for some reason she was unable to tell him to stop. He sniffed her hair theatrically, then let out a "mmmmm." Alice managed to get herself twisted around so that her shoulder was now against his chest, the better to push him away. The older coworker was giggling and clapping; the younger sat mutely, looking sick.

"I have to pee," she said, in panic and shock. At that he freed her, and she staggered down the narrow hall to the bathroom.

Immediately she understood her mistake. He would be waiting for her in that thin and out-of-the-way corridor.

She forced herself to pee. While she did she fumbled with her phone. She knew she should call Scott, call Sadie, call her mother, call anyone to come rescue her. But she could not put the words together, could not manage to make the situation as dire in her conscious mind as it felt in her body. He couldn't do anything to her, she told herself. He couldn't. There were laws, rules. He was an old man. She tried to tell herself that she was being silly, but she could not be convinced.

She washed her hands, feeling panic building. The bathroom window was small and high up in the wall. Still she considered it.

He was right there when she came out, leaning slightly, stinking of whiskey.

"I've gotta go home," she said.

"I got a home we can go to," he said. He moved fast for his age, faster than she could react. He pulled her by her hip and swung her around so that her back was pressed fully against his chest. Casually, as though he did it all the time, he forced his hand down her panties and fingered her vagina. At this she shrieked, elbowed him in the gut, and pulled away.

"Well," he said, rubbing moisture between his thumb and forefinger. "Looks like you do want it."

He laughed, and she ran, out of the bar and down a street she didn't know. She stumbled and sobbed and ended up on a bus stop bench. For a long while she sat and cried. A bus pulled up and the driver looked at her expectantly. She hesitated for a second, then waved him away. She reached into her purse and called an Uber to take her back to her car at work. She was terrified that he would be there when she arrived, but the parking lot was deserted. She drove home and on the ride she went blank and distant and couldn't quite keep the assault in the center of her attention.

At home she showered, the water scalding. She called the office and left a voicemail saying she was sick and couldn't come in tomorrow, but would be sure to be right on time the next day. She dressed herself in baggy and formless clothing, an oversized T-shirt, a pair of Scott's athletic shorts. She robotically put on YouTube and half-watched for another hour. Then it was time for bed.

She went into the bathroom and pulled her pill bottles down from the medicine cabinet. Their transparent orange material looked sickly to her, reminded her of hospitals and other places where people went to die. She opened the lithium and studied a single pill, its sickly white color, the tiny letter engraved on its side. She looked out her own tiny little bathroom window and saw nothing but asphalt and cars. She gazed down the drain in her sink. It looked, she thought, rather inviting, a tunnel that led far away.

Fifteen

Hunted, she roamed barefoot on hot Oklahoma City streets. Behind her the wolves followed, persistent but unhurried. The bars she passed were a riot of light and noise. In front of one a pack of hulking and malevolent figures stood and stumbled and shout-spoke to each other. They cackled at her as she approached. One of them reached out and pawed at her. She raked his neck with her fingernails, drawing four perfect lines of blood. He recoiled and shouted and his friends shouted and she ran until she was sure no one was following her.

Beating, beating, beating staccato out of her chest, her heart kept the same rhythm as her feet. The sky looked vast and unknowable but it attracted her gaze nonetheless; the ground held people, stalking, seeing people. The trumpets were playing again, shrill and insistent and impossibly loud. She stumbled onward, sure that to stop was to die. All she saw on the streets around her were the gaunt and lusting faces of wicked men. She had to run. Her feet were now bleeding, thanks to the jagged detritus that littered the streets. But she had to run.

Eventually she came to the park. Its grass was soothing on her aching feet and she was drawn to the sound of the water flowing over the dam. She crept out onto the walkway and peered over. It looked inviting, and for a long moment she held herself completely still. But the sounds of footsteps reignited her animal instincts and she ran.

She circled around the lake, which looked vast and cold. She peered into it, searching for something. She thought that she might like walking straight in better than diving onto the bare metal of the dam. She might have stayed and looked, or she might have gone in, but she did neither because of the bird, because she saw the bird.

She saw the great blue heron out of the corner of her eye, then rotated to her left, achingly slowly; they were skittish animals. The heron was moving slowly in that odd gait of theirs, moving silently on delicate stilts. And it terrified her. Not because of what it was, a five-foot-tall bird with a sharp beak for spearing fish and rats, tall thin legs that bent backwards, dinosaur face and more feathers than one bird should reasonably possess. She was not afraid of any of that; she had seen them in this very park before. No, it was where the heron was hunting that sent a spasm shivering up her neck. It was standing at least a hundred feet from the water's edge, on dry ground, away from its natural place but seemingly unconcerned. And for dark distant indescribable reasons Alice saw this and felt sheer terror.

The bird stood looking at her, and she stood looking at it. She shivered in the Oklahoma heat. What was that bird to do with earth, with dry ground? What had compelled it to walk as she walked on grass where children picnicked? What secrets did it hold about her, about her future? Its alien head twitched to the right, peering at her from the other eye. Alice stood transfixed, soaking with sweat, feet bleeding, assaulted by waves of fear so palpable she could feel them pressing against her physically, materially, corporeally. What was the bird doing on the grass? Why had its prehistoric feet chosen to walk on ground that had been plotted by the fickle needs of men? What did it know?

Then she knew what the bird knew: that she didn't have much time left to run, that flashing red and blue lights were ahead of her, that her future was a padded room, a cell, a cage.

Sixteen

She had somehow made it two more days in that state before she was strapped to a gurney again. The new hospital had been colder and less friendly than the first, and the first was not warm, but there was something spartan about it that fit with her need to get well. It was in therapy at the hospital that she first told anyone about what her superior at work had done to her at that bar; the therapist, a woman not much older than herself, told her that it was a great trauma and a terrible crime. And this became what they would work on together, all session, every session. Alice seldom stopped to think that the bigger problem long preceded that night. It would have felt like a betrayal of the therapist to do so. Because it had been a great trauma and a terrible crime, and Alice was never one to be ungrateful.

She had hung on to that job for months afterward, shrinking and cringing and hiding in the bathroom from her boss's boss. She simply couldn't see how she could survive losing her job, financially, and the thought of going to the HR department seemed a pointless and cruel prospect. He was, after all, friends with everyone in the building. At least that young coworker who had witnessed what happened quit a few weeks later; she liked to think he had done it out of respect for her. But she herself held on.

In the end it was not her focus or memory that did her in. Freed from the chemical prison of her meds, her brain gradually sped up again over time. She shed weight and she chewed through books and her apartment had never been cleaner. It was only a matter of time till the paranoia took her and she came to see dark conspiracies all around. Eventually she sent the wrong sort of email to a coworker, another young woman, and that was that. It was one of the warnings she would sometimes send out, when she was in that state—dark, vague, ringed with implicit violence. Her boss was just about ready to cut her loose anyway and a bizarre and threatening email to a colleague was more than enough for HR. In the weeks that followed she spent her meager savings and wrote furiously in her notebooks about inscrutable threats and her grandiose plans. She had not told her parents and could not talk to Sadie at all, as Sadie had developed a keen sense about Alice's moods. She had dozens of unread texts and unanswered calls from Sadie. By that night she saw the bird, her parents, too, were leaving concerned messages, but they were easily ignored, and when they drove up to her apartment in fear for her safety they found her gone, hospitalized. It took an entire day of panicked phone calls for them to discover where Alice was being sent.

That she had avoided Sadie for fear of appearing sick did not mean she wasn't. The doctors called it anosognosia, the inability of the mentally ill to understand that they are mentally ill. She was told that it was very common in schizophrenics, and thus it was an assumed part of psychosis in popular culture, but like most who suffered as Alice suffered she did not have it. Her first break had left her so animalistic and terrified that she perhaps did not have conscious thoughts enough to audit her own condition, but in her second there was no question that she knew she was sick. She knew she was mentally ill; she knew she suffered from delusions. She knew. The trouble was that she knew these things with no more force or certainty than she knew that friends were reading her emails, that old lovers were stealing her money, that strangers on the streets were waiting for an opportunity to poison her food. Her mind was operating; it was just operating on bad information. No, she knew that she was sick, in that second episode. Just like she knew it during the third, which arrived some nine months later.

She moved back in with her parents after getting out of the hospital; she was broke and could do little else. She knew her father had to pay thousands to her landlord to get her out of the lease early. She felt shame about that, and about much else.

At first her mother insisted on watching Alice take her meds. This went on for weeks. Alice's mother was fundamentally kind, however, and given to a certain odd flavor of libertarian parenting, and anyway she preferred denial to vigilance. So six months after Alice's second breakdown, six wasted months of job hunting and reading and denying Scott's proposals, she stopped taking her meds again. For a couple months, life felt vast and exciting again. And then she was psychotic.

It was during the run up to that third episode, in those days when it was early enough that she was still somewhat composed but late enough that she was energetic and vivacious, that she lost Scott. He took her second episode with his usual steady calm, came and visited her in the hospital, spent more time at her house when her parents wanted her close. He was reliable and boring and could usually make her come, and though she had no interest in moving in together, let alone marriage, she didn't want to lose him. But she did lose him.

She went to a friend's birthday party without Scott, who had a family function to attend. It was a rare social event; she was nervous, but both her therapist and her parents were urging her to be more social. She found it oddly comforting to hang out with people from high school again, and though she had expected everyone to treat her differently because her struggles were so public, most of them were natural and cool. As she drank hard seltzer she became more and more outgoing, cracked more jokes, told more salacious stories, and the people around her seemed to love it. And deep inside her the fires were firing and pushing her further and further up.

So when an old friend of hers and a girl she didn't know started arguing about who could give the best lap dance, she of course butted in and insisted that it was her. And they laughed and shouted and demonstrated some of their best moves, and eventually of course a boy there said that no one could tell without a real lap to dance in, and he volunteered himself. He was handsome and thick and dumb in the way Alice liked, and so she immediately jumped on his lap and grinded on him, felt his erection in his pants, turned around and rubbed her ample ass on his crotch. People cheered and clapped, but when she got up the other girls just said, "You win," and the vibe changed and she knew she had ruined everything. Later on that boy would try to drag her to his truck. "I have a boyfriend," she said, and drove straight home, not saying goodbye to anyone.

The damage was done. Someone at the party took a video of her, and they had posted it to Instagram. When Sadie texted her about it and she watched the video she cried big wet tears; she would never cheat on her boyfriend. She had merely been demonstrating her skills, embracing one of the very few sparks of competitive spirit she had felt in a life spent acquiescing to her own mediocrity. But when she sent the video to Scott as a peremptory move, an attempt to save the relationship, he had told her simply that it was over. She screamed and cried into her phone, and she reminded him that he had asked if she was a slut while having sex a thousand times, and she had always said yes, and he had always responded with grunting approval. But it was useless. He said she had betrayed him, and watching the video again she knew it was true. And so someone who had been a steadying and affectionate presence in her life for years was lost, and Alice knew he was right to go.

Now she was staring down thirty, somehow, and now it was harder and harder to keep weight off. She was never getting back to her goal weight again, not without giving up on meds and falling back into all of the old bad things. She had taken to telling herself that—"This is my body, this is what it looks like," she would say, trying to prod herself into unadorned acceptance. She had been living in her own apartment for several years and her parents had permitted themselves to exhale. Her father's health had deteriorated and he could not work; now she was the one who sent them a little money each month. She got a job with the state government. It was boring office work that was not even tangentially related to what she had wanted to do, which was to work in some sort of support services for the homeless or the needy or the mentally ill. But the pay was good enough and she enjoyed the benefit of some strong workplace protections and on her second day she had strode up to the Human Resources department and filled out the forms to disclose her disability. They assured her that if a supervisor or colleague made a negative reference to her memory, focus, or fatigue, she could come to them and they would handle it. And Alice thought that it might even be true.

She had developed type II diabetes, thanks to the weight gain, which was thanks to the pills. She was still young enough and she felt she still looked attractive, but she could not secure a new boyfriend. No one ever talked to her at her job, and every man that came through the doors seemed to be fifty years old with a mustache. She scrolled and swiped through dating apps relentlessly, dating constantly, but with no success. She was too picky, maybe. She kept seeing men for three or four dates and then never hearing from them again. Sadie's theory was that she was giving too many blowjobs.

"You can't keep giving guys head after a second date! They'll think you're too slutty to date seriously."

Alice didn't have the heart to tell Sadie that she did slutty things not to impress men but because they gave her pleasure. Anyway, she rejected as many men as rejected her. She was forever picturing whether she could someday sit at her breakfast table and tell the guy of the day about her condition, about her pills, about her episodes. She never could. Like most people Alice could not imagine that a person who did not love her now might grow to love her in time.

She had a little condo in a suburban corner of Oklahoma City. She went to movies alone, sometimes, and wasn't afraid to sit at a restaurant bar with a book, eating dinner and drinking a single beer. She had a work friend named Jackie and they would gossip and get coffee together, but their friendship never made that difficult and crucial step into the world of hanging out away from work. But it was all right. Sooner or later a man would come along, and with a man would come kids, and kids would mean other parents, and her life would be a riot of toys and diapers and little child feet, harried Christmas nights wrapping presents, getting slightly drunk at some other family's birthday party. She thought of this life every single day. Domesticity was her last, best dream. She had no other ambitions.

She was already running up against the limits of how high she might rise in her agency's hierarchy. Her attention and focus problems persisted. Her boss was a kind career public servant who had been informed of her medications and their side effects and did what she could to shield Alice from criticism. But it was one thing to provide an accommodation against active discrimination and a far different thing to see leadership potential in someone. There was no heavy hand of a denial, no one explicitly telling her that she would not rise higher. She just kept bumping her head against the realities of the job she had, the one she could get.

She joined an online support group for people like her. It drove her crazy, but she felt that doing it was an important part of her penance. There were too many people, and as had happened in every group therapy session and support group the same few seemed to dominate discussion every week. She was perpetually annoyed at their endlessly splintering diagnoses; it seemed like every one of them had to have their own boutique way of describing what was at heart the same shared problem. But when her time came to check in, she dutifully looked into her webcam, talked about how she was tolerating her meds, jokingly lamented about the side effects, and said that overall, she was doing fine. And so she was.

But people who are fine can still have things they need to excavate, and so after work every Thursday she hurried to therapy. Her boss looked the other way while she left a half-hour early; still, she often missed the first five or ten minutes of her sessions, time which her therapist of course did not credit her back. Today she would make it.

Getting into therapy in the first place had been a nightmare, as it always was. She was now in the biggest city in the state, which would seem to offer her plenty of choices. It did not. Many or most therapists did not take insurance, at all, and out-of-pocket she had been quoted two hundred and fifty dollars an hour or more. The search function on her insurance's webpage turned up dozens of potential choices, but it was permanently out of date, and anyway even most therapists who accepted her insurance were not accepting new patients, an element of searching for mental healthcare that never seemed to occur to most people. Nor did the therapists who were accepting new patients have any obligation to set their appointments in a way that would fit with her work schedule; when they would, say, offer her Monday mornings at 10:30 a.m. and she would say that this wouldn't fly with her boss, the response was always the same—take it or leave it.

The biggest problem was that many therapists simply had no interest in working with patients with a psychotic disorder. She had called many offices and, when asked to talk about her condition, been straightforward about her history, only to be told that she should "find a therapist who better fits her needs." She had done intake appointments where she laid out all of the many various elements of her history and her traumas and her life, and at the end they had thanked her quietly. Then they would call a few days later and tell her that she needed to find a therapist who better fit her needs. They did, of course, charge her insurance. And so though she was somewhat dissatisfied with the woman she had found, she knew she had little choice.

She hustled into the therapist's office, which sat in a drab business park but was soothing inside. She arrived early enough that she could sit in a comfy chair and scratch the little rake around in the sand in one of those Zen gardens. Before she knew it they were calling her in.

Her therapist was a small spare intimidating woman. She had many degrees and the diplomas hung on the wall to prove it. She was kind in the way of therapists, that distant sort of kindness, like someone waving to you from the far side of a lake. She smiled and nodded as Alice walked in, and she lifted her hand to indicate the chair where Alice should sit, as she had every session for months.

They began with the usual. Alice was to tell her about her week. It was the usual litany: she was fatigued, from the pills; she hated her body; she worried over her father; she was horny but picky; she was stressed about money. These things didn't change.

What also didn't change was how her therapist steered the discussion—ceaselessly into her childhood, relentlessly into her distant past.

"Let's return to primary school," she said, in that typical therapist manner that left Alice wondering if the woman had even bothered to listen to the preamble.

"I don't know how much else I have to say," said Alice.

"I find it's useful to tell the same stories multiple times," said the therapist. "It's good to find what changes and what stays the same."

"All right," said Alice. Memory was a sore spot and she hated to cater to the idea that she had misremembered something. But she remembered a favorite saying from Gerard, of all people, from her first hospitalization: Work the program. So she answered.

She talked about her parents, her home, her street, their cul-de-sac, her little bike with pink streamers. She talked about the local public schools she attended, her friends there, her enemies. She talked about a life spent knowing she was unexceptional. She talked about Sadie and her old friend Emma, who had more or less cut ties with everyone the day they graduated high school. She described her basic, uncomplicated childhood, told her therapist that it was not some bucolic dream but also not especially hard. And then they came to the sticking point. The therapist squirmed a little in her chair, which she always did when she was dissatisfied with something Alice had said.

"We still need to get to the roots," she said. "If we're going to help you reach another stage of managing your condition, we need to find its origins."

Alice stifled a sigh. It was always the same. The talk of "another stage" was standard issue too; the doctors and therapists were always careful to hedge their bets, never to talk of a final victory, never ever to speak of a cure. Instead the goal was always to climb some invisible ladder of treatment, the rungs of which seemed totally arbitrary. All they ever knew about the climb was that it only ever went upward, that Alice was proceeding higher and higher, every day, toward . . . well, no one would ever say.

"I don't know," she said. "I think my childhood was alright."

"But we all have childhood traumas."

"Well, my mother's father was part of our lives when I was very young, but there was some sort of falling out and I haven't seen him since."

"Were you involved?" said the therapist.

"Involved with what?" said Alice.

"With the falling out," she said.

"I was like four years old," said Alice.

"Yes," said the therapist. "Very vulnerable."

"Oh," said Alice. "Nothing like that. It was something between my mother and grandfather. She won't ever say what it was."

"I see," said the therapist, frowning into her notepad.

And like that it went for much of the session, the therapist probing into Alice's childhood, Alice finding nothing there, the therapist sending vague notes of disapproval without ever saying anything explicitly. Finally, in the last ten minutes they talked about her assault at the bar. The therapist was sympathetic and a good listener and supported Alice throughout. But she never abandoned her agenda.

"I think for a long time after I just felt unclean," said Alice. "When I got back out of the hospital again I felt so fragile and like no one could touch me."

She was trying to circle around to the fact that she missed sex and wanted it in her life, but she found it very difficult to say that explicitly, even to a therapist.

"Have you felt that way before?" asked the therapist. "Unclean?"

And so it went, always. Soon their fifty minutes had passed and Alice was thanking the therapist and saying goodbye.

Before heading home she visited a quiet café where she could sit outside. She ordered an iced chai latte and got a choice seat near the entrance. Dry heat hung in the air but under the shade of her table's umbrella she felt comfortable. She pulled out her book, a thick historical novel, and read from it in spurts and batches. Reading was no easier than it had been previously, thanks to the meds, but she had set herself a goal of becoming a reader once more and she was pleased to find that she had stuck with it. Her psychiatrist had told her to let go of the dream of uninterrupted reading and to accept that reading would be a piecemeal, slow-going process.

"Allow yourself to accept that model of reading, of writing, of anything," he had said. "Stop comparing your focus or memory to that of your old self."

She had taken to seeing him as a wise sage. It felt easiest, that way. Her time in the mental health system had revealed the abundant failures of doctors. But she had had to surrender to someone, so she surrendered to the wisdom of this kind man who she mostly saw through her laptop screen.

"Your ex-lover is dead," he once said of her old self, her unmedicated self. "Move on the way you would move on from an old boyfriend." And that too was wise.

Sitting there in front of that café, nursing an overly-expensive drink, watching mothers feed their children and couples on awkward dates, she thought of that phrase like a mantra—her ex-lover was dead. There was nothing to think about. She felt nothing and thus had no past. She was free. Her therapist's endless searching into her childhood, leaving her feeling like the man locked in a dark cell repetitively searching on hands and knees for a pin, to stay occupied and stave off madness, was only an exercise. She rode the probing out the way she rode out the shakes, the sweating, the diarrhea, the loneliness, the cold mornings stuffing too many pills in her mouth. She was working the program and she was alive.

Seventeen

She was off her pills again but she was not yet in the thick of things; she could feel the medications washing themselves out of her body but she was not climbing that same exhausting staircase inside herself. But if she did nothing, she knew, it would come.

Thirty-six years old, friendless, now jobless. Even her Sadie was gone now, lost to yet another string of accusations, sobbing phone calls, brutal insults, and silence. She had finally pushed with enough force, talked with enough cruelty, that she had chased off her last friend; it had been accomplished. Even Sadie was gone. Even her Sadie.

Her father was dead. Without him her mother had descended into a visible delicacy; when Alice saw her she feared she might blow away in the wind. Something within her mother had given, and she was old, suddenly old. Alice held doors open for her, now. She called her when there was a heavy rain and she called her when there was a news story that was likely to upset her. Her mother had been the greatest source of Alice's stability, and then overnight she became Alice's responsibility. The weight of it hung heavily on her and she worried constantly, and she knew that her next episode might finish her mother. But still and all she had gone off meds.

There was no great precipitating incident this time. It was simply the collection of gray days, living on disability payments that would not last, trudging down to the library to look for jobs, turning her ancient car's engine over and over until it would start. She was fat now, properly fat, her face lined with crow's feet and laugh lines, and she saw a stranger in the mirror. The side effects wore on her as they always did, even the minor ones feeling ever-amplified by the passage of years, but that wasn't the reason she had stopped. Not the weight, not the brain fog, not the shakes, not the shits, not the disinterest in sex. No, she stopped because she could no longer bear the physical act of taking the pills. Just that and only that—year after numbing year of opening the bottles, measuring out the pills, placing them in her mouth, taking a sip of water, and swallowing—had left her bitter and exhausted. That was what she could not take anymore, that was what she felt moved to reject. She never wanted to experience it again, the taste of chalk, the slight choking sensation of the oversized pills, the ritual that brought no relief.

And so she thought she might take some pills, one last time.

She had prepared for the occasion. She had strategically manipulated her doctor into giving her a prescription for amitriptyline, an older antidepressant that was used less often than SSRIs now and mostly given to those whose depression had resisted other treatments. But she had no interest in its antidepressant effects, in fact had no intention of waiting around to see what the effects were. She had chosen it because it was known to commonly cause death through overdose. How much would it take, five pills, ten, fifteen? She couldn't say, so she would take them all. She would chase them down with half a bottle of hydrocodone, left over from a bad fall she had taken down the stairs a year prior; when the hospital had called her mother, she had assumed immediately that Alice was having another episode, but in fact she had merely been clumsy, perhaps thanks to the influence of the shakes and rattles her pills gave her. If all else failed, she would take her little orange utility knife to her wrists, the one she had bought for a short-lived attempt at scrapbooking.

What would she look like when they found her? She figured she would be sprawled out awkwardly on her coffee table, spit caking her lower chin and her lips turned a grayish blue, like a blue in stained glass, the color of a bruise.

She poured herself a glass of wine and put on her and Sadie's old favorite song, the one that was popular the summer after junior year, the one they would blast in Sadie's little convertible as they sped down the highway, wanting for nothing. She listened for sixty seconds and then turned it off; she scrolled through her music, looking for something appropriately somber. She thought of her mother and what might happen to her. She knew she was being selfish. But that guilt only made her more desperate to get to a place where she would not feel shame or guilt at all.

Shame. Unyielding, endless shame. Shame was the water in which she swam. She was buffeted by it, drowning in it. She couldn't move, couldn't act, couldn't speak without provoking it in her. She thought of them all, all of the friends, the boyfriends, her poor parents, all of the people who had loved her and paid a price for it. She had lived in shame now for some sixteen years. She thought of one of those poor boyfriends who she had subjected to her typical pattern of escalating paranoia, increasingly theatrical demands, and eventual infidelity.

"The worst part," he said as he walked out of her apartment for the last time, "is that you'll never feel sorry."

She would, though, feel sorry, sooner or later, but he could be forgiven for thinking otherwise. Because she never would feel sorry while she was in that state; when her condition was in full bloom, when she was walking with celestial beings through a hallway of paranoia and delusion, she might very well remember that she was sick, understand that the crash was coming—but she would never feel sorry. Sorry came after, when she was medicated again. That was the worst side effect, and the cruelest element of all. To enter treatment again was to feel waves of unrelenting guilt for what she did when she was not in treatment. The only time she enjoyed her life was when she was in the process of destroying it.

She grabbed her bathroom trash can and positioned it near her, in case she needed to vomit, and poured herself a glass of water. She had initially planned to do it in the bathtub, but she was afraid that her downstairs neighbor's ceiling might flood. She sat down on her beaten-up couch and tried to think of some ceremony she might perform, but came up empty. Even her mother no longer went to church. She supposed she might as well get to it.

Then she found that she was deviating from the plan. Motivated by some stray impulse, she went to the bathroom again and fetched her pills, the ones she was meant to take. She brought them back to the table and with something like reverence placed them down one by one on the table, opposite from the deadly pills. When she set them down, she realized that this was the pageantry she was looking for. She would ceremonially choose to die over choosing her medications. It was all a little pretentious and theatrical, but she had afforded herself so little self-importance over the years, and the world had provided her with so little of the organic kind. In a life in which she had permitted herself no pretensions, in a life in which she had always known that she was not one of those who was entitled to see their life as a beautiful journey, she would allow herself this, this last attempt to inject poetry into whatever was left of her time. She had earned it, and no one else would ever know.

And then, as perhaps some part of her brain predicted, the choice suddenly did not seem ceremonial. Suddenly she was faced with the choice, itself, and it didn't seem pretentious at all. It just seemed exhausting to a perpetually exhausted woman.

For the last time, she thought of running unencumbered on hot nights, skinny ankles, a total lack of inhibitions, a foul and funny mouth, unapologetic but pleasantly shameful sex with whomever she pleased, the energy, the flow, the flood of feeling, the intensity that surpassed any understanding. For the last time in her life she thought enviously of the periods in which she had taken everything she had and set it all on fire. And then she thought of Clara, of the army of Claras she had compiled in a particularly shameful roster, good people who she had hurt and driven away, and she let it all go, at once. Bare feet on city pavement sounded nice. But she was alone, and she deserved to be. She knew that she faced a simple choice: to learn to live like this, with the meds, with the weight, with the shits, with the shakes, with the brain full of holes, with the muted emotions, in the quiet dull spaces in which the healthy mind lives, or else to die.

She thought of the life she still might salvage, a decent man with kind eyes, a job she could tolerate, a modest home close to her mother, work that she didn't hate, perhaps even work that permitted her to see the face of real human beings she was really helping, quiet spaces of her own, people who understood and accepted her condition, and Sadie back, Sadie won back with apology, total and unqualified apology, with humble entreaties and with time. On top of that, a child perhaps, another life to live for, tiny little shoes for tiny little feet, teaching them to swim, trips to see grandma, "the cow goes moo," bruised knees, walks in the park, the continuation of some small part of herself, but only the good part. She still wanted so badly to pour herself down the drain in her sink, to go to the place where there was no mind in which to be trapped, where all of her paranoid fears would be lost in the blanketing dark; she could not picture a future in which she never had another episode. She could not bring herself to do that. It was beyond her most romantic imagining. And so the deadly pills called to her, and so too did the cool sharp edge of her utility knife, machined not to harm but to complete a necessary task. But, perhaps, she could imagine a future where she got sick and then got well again, and where she would then be forgiven. Perhaps she could imagine a world where, someday, she forgave herself. Perhaps she could imagine a world where her shame was only a neighbor that stopped by from time to time, an acquaintance with whom she would break bread, a strange kind of friend with whom she might share tea. Perhaps she could be forgiven. Perhaps she could be forgiven. Perhaps she could be forgiven.

Before her on the coffee table sat two sets of orange pill bottles. She had held hundreds like them before and hated every one. But at that moment she was taken by their mundane beauty; sunlight streaming through her dirty windows lit their tops like humble prisms and cast little beams of amber on the table. Within them rested two different types of medication, now intended for two very different purposes, though the bottles themselves were exactly alike, machined in rugged plastic. Alice knew she had to decide which bottle to open, which of the various two-toned capsules to take, whether to swallow only once more or again and again forever, knew she had to weigh one against the other, and to choose. So she did.

Coffee House Press began as a small letterpress operation in 1972 and has grown into an internationally renowned nonprofit publisher of literary fiction, essay, poetry, and other work that doesn't fit neatly into genre categories.

LITERATURE
is not the same thing as
PUBLISHING

Funder Acknowledgments

Coffee House Press is an internationally renowned independent book publisher and arts nonprofit based in Minneapolis, MN; through its literary publications, Coffee House acts as a catalyst and connector—between authors and readers, ideas and resources, creativity and community, inspiration and action.

Coffee House Press books are made possible through the generous support of grants and donations from corporations, state and federal grant programs, family foundations, and the many individuals who believe in the transformational power of literature. This activity is made possible by the voters of Minnesota through a Minnesota State Arts Board Operating Support grant, thanks to the legislative appropriation from the Arts and Cultural Heritage Fund. Coffee House also receives major operating support from the Amazon Literary Partnership, McKnight Foundation, and the National Endowment for the Arts (NEA). To find out more about how NEA grants impact individuals and communities, visit www.arts.gov.

Coffee House Press receives additional support from Bookmobile; the Buckley Charitable Fund; Dorsey & Whitney LLP; and the Schwab Charitable Fund.

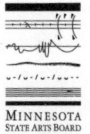

The Publisher's Circle of Coffee House Press

Publisher's Circle members make significant contributions to Coffee House Press's annual giving campaign. Understanding that a strong financial base is necessary for the press to meet the challenges and opportunities that arise each year, this group plays a crucial part in the success of Coffee House's mission.

Recent Publisher's Circle members include many anonymous donors, Patricia A. Beithon, Robin Chemers Neustein, Kelli Cloutier, Theodore Cornwell, Jane Dalrymple-Hollo, Jeremy M. Davies, Mary Ebert and Paul Stembler, Kamilah Foreman, Eva Galiber, Bryan Garrett, Roger Hale and Nor Hall, William Hardacker, Randy Hartten and Ron Lotz, Carl and Heidi Horsch, Amy L. Hubbard and Geoffrey J. Kehoe Fund of the St. Paul & Minnesota Foundation, Hyde Family Charitable Fund, Kenneth & Susan Kahn, the Kenneth Koch Literary Estate, Cinda Kornblum, the Lenfestey Family Foundation, Carol and Aaron Mack, Gillian McCain, Mary and Malcolm McDermid, Daniel N. Smith III and Maureen Millea Smith, Vance Opperman, Mr. Pancks' Fund in memory of Graham Kimpton, Alan Polsky, Robin Preble, Ronald Restrepo and Candace S. Baggett, Elizabeth Schnieders, Steve Smith, Jeffrey Sugerman and Sarah Schultz, Paul Thissen, Allyson Tucker, Grant Wood, Margaret Wurtele, Aptara Inc., The Buckley Charitable Fund, Dorsey and Whitney Foundation.

For more information about the Publisher's Circle and other ways to support Coffee House Press books, authors, and activities, please visit www.coffeehousepress.org/pages/donate or contact us at info@coffeehousepress.org.

FREDRIK DEBOER is a writer and academic. His writing has appeared in *The New York Times, The Los Angeles Times, The Washington Post, The Boston Globe, Playboy,* and *Harper's* among many others. His nonfiction books include *How Elites Ate the Social Justice Movement* (2023) and *The Cult of Smart* (2020). He holds a PhD in English with a concentration in writing assessment and higher education policy from Purdue University. He lives in Connecticut with his wife, his son Junho, and his cat Suavecito.

The Mind Reels was designed by
Bookmobile Design & Digital Publisher Services.
Text is set in Adobe Caslon Pro.